THREE DAYS
IN
WINTER

Books in
The Jennifer Grey Mystery Series

THREE DAYS IN WINTER

A
Jennifer Grey
Mystery

Jerry B. Jenkins

AMERSHAM-ON-THE-HILL, BUCKS HP6 6JQ
ENGLAND

© 1986 Jerry B. Jenkins

This book was first published in the United States by Moody Press. Copyright 1986 by Jerry B. Jenkins

Scripture Press Foundation Edition printed by permission of Moody Bible Institute, Chicago, Il.

First British edition 1990

ISBN 1 872059 15 5

Production and Printing in England for
SCRIPTURE PRESS FOUNDATION (UK) LTD
Raans Road, Amersham-on-the-Hill, Bucks HP6 6JQ by
Nuprint Ltd, 30b Station Road, Harpenden, Herts AL5 4SE.

1 Heather Lauren. Jennifer thought it was a beautiful name, a name you might find in the social register of a debutante. Not the name of a murder victim on a police blotter in the West Side Precinct station.

'But that's where I found it,' she told her boss, *Chicago Day* City Editor Leo Stanton. 'The cops don't like it.'

'I don't like it either,' the veteran editor said, the ever-present unlit cigar jammed in his teeth. 'Four years old? Where'd they find her?'

'Tied in the cellar.'

'Abused?'

'Beaten, burned. Malnourished.'

Leo swore. 'Burned?'

Jennifer nodded, her eyes filling with tears.

Leo shook his head. 'I've seen almost everything in this business,' he said. 'In fact, I've seen this kinda thing before. But I never get used to it.' He stood and walked around to the front of his desk, leaning back against it and crossing his arms as he stared down at Jennifer. 'What're you going to do with it?'

She pressed her lips tight. 'I don't know,' she said, just above a whisper. 'Play it straight, I guess. Quote the cops. Try to recreate how she was found. Talk to the coroner, the neighbours, check with Social Services.'

Leo Stanton rolled up his sleeves and tugged at the waistband of his slipover. He closed his eyes and let his head fall back, then reached up and slowly took off his half glasses, gently placing them on the desk beside him. 'What would you do with this story if you could do whatever you wanted?' he asked.

Jennifer dropped her head and stared into her lap for several seconds. 'I saw the pictures, Leo,' she said.

'Hm?'

'The photographs of Heather Lauren. Martin Grom, the Homicide Detective Sergeant on the West Side, showed them to me. I almost wish he hadn't.'

'I know Grom. A good guy, right? Big man. A redhead.'

'That's him.'

'Gruesome photos, huh? Nothing we can use, I s'pose.'

'We could use one, but not the other. She was a doll, Leo. Apparently the only good picture her mother had of her was taken at some local Park District function. The kids brought the pictures home to see if the parents wanted to buy them. Some did. Some kept them without buying them. That's what Mrs. Lauren did.'

'And we can get that picture?'

'Sure.'

'Get it.'

'Even that picture makes me sick, Leo. It's so precious it makes me think of the horrible one I saw in Grom's office. Do I have to describe it?'

'To me? No. I don't get any more kick out of something like that than you do. In your piece, yes. The reader has to know what happened, Jennifer. You know that.'

She nodded, still staring down. The old man put a hand on her shoulder. 'Jennifer, you never answered my question, so I'm gonna answer it for you. I want you to whip out the straight story fast. We'll go with it on page one with the good photo. Then I want you to do a sidebar; anything you want.'

'Oh, Leo, no. You won't print what I'd have to write.'

'You're gonna tell me what I'd print?' he said, smiling. 'Try me.'

'It's not funny, Leo. It's just that I'm so angered by this thing that I don't know if I can even do the straight story without intruding on it.'

'You know I can't print opinion in the straight piece, Jennifer. And I can't have you spouting off about your religion. But a little emotion, especially on a story like this, well, there's no harm in that. That's why I'm telling you to do two. Let *me* decide if I can print the sidebar or not. Regardless, the page one story has to be done within the hour, and you'd better send someone to the West Side to get that photograph. I don't s'pose we can scoop the *Trib* or the *Times* on the photo.'

'No, but at least we won't be the only one without it, and that's saying something.'

'That's saying something, all right,' Stanton said, returning to his chair. 'The *Trib* has Bob Greene and Dear Abby. The *Times* has Mike Royko and Gary Deeb. We're glad when we're not the only one *without* a hot photo. The only thing we've got is the best police reporter in town.'

Jennifer would have enjoyed the compliment another day. Now she trudged to the video screen at her desk, sliding her leather shoulder bag to the floor and draping her calf-length camel-hair coat over the back of the chair.

It was always hot in the newsroom. She unzipped her boots and sat in stocking feet, digging from her bag the spiral notebook containing her notes. She propped it up next to the screen, then called the West Side Precinct station house.

'Chicago Police.'

'Homicide, please.'

'Jis' a minute.'

'Homicide, Henry.'

'Sergeant Grom, please.'

'He's busy. Can he call you back?'

'No, please tell him it's Jennifer Grey from the *Day*.'

'Grey from the *Day* for Grom on the phone? I love it! Hang on.'

'This is Grom. Hi, Jenn.'

'Hi, Martin. Listen, I know you're in the middle of this thing, but can I send someone to get the picture?'

'Yeah. You wanted the Park District shot, right?'

'Of course. You're not releasing the one from the cellar, are you?'

'You want it?'

'No, but —'

'Your competitors want it.'

'You're kidding!'

'Nope. They both want it.'

'They going to run it?'

'You mean do they want to? I can't imagine. I'd never let it out. Would you want that photo in the paper if it was your kid?'

Jennifer thought she heard an edge in Martin Grom's voice she hadn't heard before. 'You're in a bad mood, aren't you?' she tried.

'Ah,' he said, pausing. 'I got a young daughter myself. If I had it *my* way, I'd kill Wyatt Oliver right now.'

Jennifer reached for her notebook so fast she knocked it to the floor. 'You're saying you believe Cornelia Lauren's common-law husband murdered the child?'

'Oh, Jenn, you can't quote me on that, please! Can't I just spout off to you without getting my neck in a noose? I'd be assigned to the mayor's office for pest control if that came out in the paper.'

'That didn't sound off-the-record to me, Martin. You know you have to tell me it's off-the-record *before* you say it, not after.'

'Well, you gotta pretend I told you in time on this one, Jennifer. Don't pull any technicality on me and quote me just because I felt free to tell you what I was thinking. Promise me.'

'You don't have to worry, Martin. Hang on a second so I can tell Bobby to go and get the picture.'

She signalled to her assistant, Robert Block, who sat with his feet up on his desk reading *Newsweek*.

'West Side Precinct,' she said. 'An envelope is in my name at the desk. Get it to the composing room ASAP.'

'Why didn't you get it when you were there?' he whined.

'They had to make copies for each of us — oh, Bobby, just hit the road, will you? Do I have to tell Leo that you're being —'

'No, but I have no doubt that you would, with half a reason.'

'You waste any time getting that photo, and I'll have more than half a reason.' She turned back to the phone. 'Sorry, Martin. So, tell me, is Mrs. Lauren sticking with her story, or did she lead you to believe that this, uh, Oliver, uh, Wyatt Oliver guy killed Heather?'

'You're not gonna print what I said, right?'

'I promised, Martin.'

'Awright. No, both she and Oliver are sticking with their story.'

'And what you don't like about it is that if

10

the daughter had really been missing for two days, they would have reported it to somebody?'

'Right.'

'OK, Martin, off-the-record. If Wyatt Oliver killed the kid, why would his common-law wife cover for him?'

''Cause she's scared to death of him. Wouldn't you be?'

Jennifer thought for a moment. 'I guess so. I'd rather not say how I feel about him right now, because I'm afraid you're right.'

'We just want to book him soon, because there's another kid in the family — you know, the seven-year-old boy.'

'Elliott?'

'Right.'

'Is that his real name?'

'Yeah, Elliott Lauren.'

'Another beautiful name for a poor, sad child.'

'Yeah, I gotta go, Jenn. I'll call you if I get anything more.'

'No you won't.'

'You're right, I prob'ly won't. But I do owe ya one. You don't print what I said about Wyatt Oliver, and I may just call you if I get anything new.'

'Thanks, Martin.'

Jennifer turned to her keyboard and began tapping out the front page story:

> The burned, beaten, and emaciated body
> of a four-year-old girl was found tied to a

post in the cellar of a West Side
apartment building Wednesday
afternoon after police responded to a call
from the girl's mother, Mrs. Cornelia
Lauren of 4326 W. Stivers. The Cook
County coroner's office is still trying to
determine the cause of death.

Mrs. Lauren, 31, who lives in the
building with her common-law husband,
Wyatt Oliver, 36, and her son, Elliott, 7,
told police her daughter Heather had not
come home from a Park District
preschool event Monday afternoon. She
said she discovered the body at
approximately 3:30 p.m. Wednesday.

West Side Homicide Detective
Sergeant Martin Grom said police had
no record of a missing person's report
having been filed in the case.
Neighbours were apparently unaware
that the girl had been missing. But
Oliver, an unemployed truck driver, says
he wouldn't have asked his neighbours
for help anyway. Oliver and Lauren are
one of few white couples in the
neighbourhood, and police have
intervened in disputes in their building
before.

When asked to explain the apparent
malnourishment, Mrs. Lauren said her
daughter had always been a light eater
and very thin. She said that whoever
had abducted the child must have
inflicted the bruises and burns, because

12

"the only time Heather ever hurt herself was when she fell down the stairs and burned herself on a hot plate."

Sergeant Grom refused to comment on any leads or suspects in the case, though he admitted that police would be questioning the couple.

Jennifer finished the article with a more detailed description of the child's injuries, along with other minor details and a menu of related articles the reader could expect over the next few days, including interviews with neighbours and acquaintances, the police, and the coroner. She transmitted the story to Leo's screen and waited.

In a few minutes her phone rang. 'Remarkably detached,' he said. 'C'mon in.'

'You can sense where my head is from the piece, though, can't you?' she asked, standing in his doorway.

"Course. So will the reader. But everyone will have the same suspicions. The kid is missing two days before the mother finds her? No one has been looking, let alone even knows the kid has been gone? The woman is a lousy liar, Jenn. She admits the kid fell down the stairs at age three — which is unlikely — and that she got burned on a hot plate. Are we talking about a burned finger? You write here that the girl had burns and burn scars on 15 per cent of her body. Maybe a kidnapper gave her the fresh burns and bruises, but burn scars? That many don't come from a hot plate unless she wrestled with the thing.'

'I know. And I'm so livid I don't even want to take a shot at the sidebar.'

'You don't understand, Jennifer,' Leo said. 'It's not a suggestion. I want that piece. If you go overboard, I'll edit you a little. Let's do it. Let's prove we know what the readers are thinking and identify with them once. People are sick and tired of people who hurt children. Let's show 'em we have the same feelings. What could you say that I wouldn't print, besides the fact that you think Jesus is the answer for everything?'

Jennifer looked pained.

'I'm sorry,' Leo said. 'That was a little cold.'

'Not to mention a little simplistic.'

'OK, guilty. But other than a sermonette, I want to see what's rattling around in your brain under all that brown hair. How 'bout it?'

2 Jennifer padded back to her desk, still not sure what to do with the sidebar and wished she could talk to Jim before their late dinner in Geneva. But she was determined to stick with the agreement she had struck with Leo and the publisher: 'You can date a police officer as long as you don't see him or talk to him when either of you are working, and provided you neither use him to gain information, nor personally handle a story in which he might be mentioned.'

It was better than being reassigned to the society page, but there were days when she wondered if it was worth it. How could she not discuss this terrible story with him, just because he happened to be a policeman? She couldn't avoid it, it was as simple as that. She loved him; she needed him as a sounding board. She wouldn't be pumping him for information, and he wouldn't offer any — not even to tip her off as to who to talk to.

Her screen's red light came on. She called up the message. 'Leo the Lion sez: Don't daydream too long. You've got about 40 minutes to give me the equivalent of 2 takes.'

'Thanks, Mane Man,' she tapped back, not feeling as light as her message. She hit the key to clear the screen and put away her notebook while the computer was doing its thing. She would do this piece off the top of her head.

She breathed a silent prayer and tried to keep her tears in check as she began:

> I saw a photograph today that made me an instant militant in the campaign for capital punishment.
>
> I don't know who beat or burned or starved or neglected four-year-old Heather Lauren to death in her own West Side basement this week, and something tells me I don't want to know.
>
> You can see the *before* picture on page one. That's her next to the grizzly headline and my just-the-facts story. If the picture were in colour, you could see that she was a blue-eyed blonde with a pageboy haircut, a shy smile, and perfect little teeth.
>
> But the beauty of the child and the horrible manner of her death is not what moves me to temporarily leave my niche as a police reporter to tell you that I feel the same way you do about this story.

I do, but then I hope you suspected that. Maybe you didn't. Maybe you think I've grown calloused over the last two years, writing about crime, about good cops and bad cops, white-collar criminals and blue-collar criminals.

Maybe you think that to me it's all just more grist for the newspaper stories, something that allows me to fill my space, justify my existence, put food on my table. Maybe you think I can forget it and go home, only to return and hit it again the next day.

Well, I can't. I'm as depressed by bad news are you are. It affects me as much. And when I've seen the police department's photo of a lifeless little body — a photo so offensive that we wouldn't dare publish it in a family newspaper — perhaps it affects me even more than it does you.

When I leave the office after writing this article, I'll go home, I'll see my friends, I'll have dinner, I'll watch the news, I'll go to bed. And when I get up, I'll come back to work and investigate the story for days until someone is suspected, sought, found, charged, convicted, and sentenced.

And then we will all forget about Heather Lauren for a while. Or will we? Will I? I'll see that picture again and again in my mind. I'll hear the story in court more times than I want to. And I'll be reminded constantly of the vulnerability of the child. Any child.

People who prey upon defenceless victims — the aged, the infirm, the young — should be punished. Of course, anyone who preys upon anyone else is wrong. But in the cases of the defenceless, the crimes are all the more heinous. For they are always perpetrated for the most selfish reasons.

Murderers murder the aged for their money. They murder the infirm for their money. They murder children for their silence, or to eliminate the haunting, hungry eyes that bring guilt. Maybe they're inconvenient.

I know this isn't the right era for tough laws, for punishment at the expense of rehabilitation, for inhumane treatment of society's misfits, for not understanding the difficult environments that produce someone capable of the crime that will be on our minds for weeks.

But if you saw the picture I saw today and compared it to the one on the front page of this newspaper, you'd be unable to swallow the lump in your throat. You'd be unable to hold back the tears. You'd be frightened of your feelings. And you'd want justice.

I can't help it. I want to see the guilty party pay for this crime. And when the bleeding heart letters come pouring in to call *me* inhumane, I'll call to memory

> that photograph just one more time and
> know I'll never change my mind.

Jennifer transmitted the story to Leo but didn't wait for his reaction. She pulled on her boots and coat and hurried down the back corridor toward the car-park, passing Bobby on the way. She sniffed and managed, 'Get it?'

'Yes, your highness,' he said. 'I can handle all dese tough jobs Massa Grey, ma'am. Anything else you wants of Bobby today?'

She ignored him and kept moving. He had tried so hard — and almost succeeded — to get her fired for seeing Jim while handling the police beat. Bobby would graduate from Northwestern University and be her boss within a few years, she guessed, unless someone was made fully aware of his attitude.

He was good at hiding it, and he *did* have unusual talent. But he was a scoundrel who needed exposing, and if she couldn't change him or at least get him to see that he needed changing, she'd have to pull him out from under his slimy rock to protect others.

This was one of those days when Bobby Block didn't seem worth the effort.

A light snow had covered Jennifer's little car, and she hated to think what she was doing to her coat, leaning against the salty, slushy sides of the car to scrape the windows. She wanted to look nice for Jim tonight. He would have been at a prayer meeting. Some day she would have an assignment that would free her to go with him. But for now, Wednesday evenings, after she got off work, were their late dinner nights.

She always looked forward to them, no matter how tired she was. And regardless of what might come up at work or how late she had to stay, Officer James Purcell would never hear of cancelling. He'd wait, he always said. And he always did. Once until eleven-thirty.

It wouldn't be that late tonight, but never had Jennifer been more tired or had more on her mind. She arrived at her apartment with just enough time to park, grab her mail, take the lift to her floor, freshen up, change her clothes, and answer the doorbell. It was too early for Jim.

'You got a delivery, Miss Grey,' old Mrs. Alexander yodelled. 'You weren't here, and I knew you weren't here, so I told him you weren't here but that I knew you and that I would take it for you and that I would even pay him, and so I did. A dollar I gave him. For this.'

Beaming, she held out a small, narrow box. Jennifer dug a dollar from her purse, deciding not to open the box until Mrs. Alexander was gone. She appreciated the kindness, but the contents of the box were none of her neighbour's business.

'Thank you very much,' Jennifer said, smiling. 'You're so kind.'

'And so is Jim,' the old woman said with a twinkle as she backed down the landing. 'One red rose, and so lovely!'

It was all Jennifer could do to keep from slamming the door.

Well, the nosy old bat was right, anyway, she said to herself, sitting on the edge of the sofa opening the box. *It is lovely.*

The card read, *I'm looking forward to tonight. Pick you up at 9.*

She nearly panicked. Was there something special about this Wednesday night? Was there something she had forgotten? Was it an anniversary of sorts? She couldn't remember. Jim was thoughtful; she'd received deliveries before. But what did his card mean? Maybe nothing, but what if she'd forgotten something she should have remembered?

She put the rose in a tiny vase and scurried to finish her face and hair. *I hope he hasn't got anything up his sleeve,* she thought, surprised by how nervous and excited she always felt about seeing him again, even after a day like today.

She knew the real thing when it came along. She'd been through it before. After other experiences of puppy love and infatuation through high school and college, she'd fallen in love with Scott Grey. And it had been only recently that she had forgiven him for dying on an icy road early in their marriage.

That was why for so long she had hidden even from herself her true feelings for Jim. It couldn't be, she decided, that the first man she chose to see after finally emerging from her grief, would be a man she could love.

And so she didn't. She simply wouldn't

allow herself to fall for him. Jim was patient. He knew. He understood. He waited. Bided his time. Proved himself. And when she had least expected it, her love for him burst from its hiding place.

She loved him unabashedly. And he loved her. They were unusually blessed with a relationship that lucky people approach only once in their lifetimes. He had been disappointed in love before. She had been happily married, then widowed. And now God had given them each other.

She looked at her watch. Eight fifty-five. Jim would arrive in five minutes, as usual. And she would be ready. As usual. She fastened her watchband and folded her coat over her arm and sat again on the edge of the couch.

She could just as easily sleep as go out, and she realized she would not go out tonight for anyone in the world but Jim. Not even Leo. Dad? She'd probably try to get out of it, but Dad could talk her into it. And if Jim was the only person besides her dad who she would go out with after an exhausting day, then that was as high a compliment as she could pay him.

She'd have done anything — and often had — for Scott too. It was good to be able to think about him rationally now. Finally. For how long had his absence been the first thing on her mind every day?

She hadn't been able to keep him from her mind, and when the memories intruded, they suffocated her with grief — longing, hoping, wishing his accident had never happened. No pleasant memory of him had ever wafted through her mind without ending in that remarkably stark and sterile conversation with the young state trooper who brought her the news that had changed her life.

Had she grown out of it, like a child who stops sucking his thumb? Had Jim taken Scott's place? No. Time, as much as she had always hated the platitude, truly had been a healer of the wound. Jim had been part of the healing process, of course, because he had not seemed threatened by her memories of Scott.

In fact, he wanted to hear about Scott. Jim felt flattered that she loved him after having been married to such an outstanding young man.

She leaped to her feet at the sound of the doorbell. There stood Jim, all tall and trim and bronze and blond, dressed in earth tones, cardigan, herringbone jacket, and open trench coat.

'Hi, Sweetheart,' he said, smiling and reaching for her.

She embraced him. 'Hi, Scott,' she said, wincing immediately and knowing he was doing the same. 'Jim, I'm so sorry. I've never done that before, have I?'

He chuckled. 'Been thinking again?'

'Yes, but mostly about you.'

'Sounds like it,' he said, still smiling.

'Really I was. I love you, Jim.'

'I love you too. Get anything from me today?'

'Yes, and I loved it. It worried me though.'

'Worried you?'

'Yes, have I forgotten something? Is there something special about this day or this dinner? If there is, I'm sorry, but it's passed me by.'

'Does it have to be a special occasion for me to remind you that I look forward to dinner with you?' he said, reaching behind her and pulling the door shut, then walking her to the lift.

'No, it's great, but if I forgot something, you remind me.'

'What would you forget?'

'The first time we held hands or kissed or something.'

'You mean we've already held hands and kissed?' he said, mocking, as the lift door shut.

She planted a passionate one on him. 'Now we have,' she said, laughing.

He wrapped his arm tightly around her as they stepped into a frigid wind. 'You look tired,' he said.

'More than usual on Wednesday night?'

'Yeah. 'Fraid so. Tough day?'

'Always.'

'But more so than usual?'

'How'd you know?'

'I know everything.'

'You know about the little girl on the West Side, of course.'

'Of course.'

'You mind if we don't talk about it?'

'Whatever you want, Jenn.' He opened the car door for her. 'I would have thought you might want to bounce it off me, though,' he said, shutting it.

'I thought so too,' she said when he slid behind the wheel. 'In fact, I've been looking forward to talking to you about it all afternoon. Now I want to talk about anything but.'

He gave her an understanding glance and pulled away into the night toward the western suburbs.

3 Jim insisted on taking Jennifer home early when she nearly dozed off at dinner. He hadn't pressed her about her reactions to the Heather Lauren murder, but she did reveal why she felt she couldn't talk about it.

'I emptied myself in a sidebar, a personal column type thing, Jim. I think the Lord really gave me clarity of mind, because it came out just the way I wanted it to. I really don't know if I could have expressed it better, and I won't try to do it from memory. You'll see it in the morning *Day*. Let me know what you think.'

'I can hardly wait. I know what I'll think. I'll think it's great, like all your stuff.'

'You don't understand, Jim. This is so forthright that it may get me into trouble with the readership. In fact, for all I know, Leo might not even print it. I all but demand capital punishment for the perpetrator.'

'You won't get any argument from my side of the street.'

'Yeah, but everybody knows you cops are right-wing red-necks. We journalists are supposed to be liberal left-wingers, remember?'

Jennifer didn't protest about the early end to the evening. It was the type of attention she appreciated so much in Jim. After praying and reading some Scripture, she mentally plotted her afternoon tasks for the next day. She'd start with the Park District preschool teacher, then contact the social worker assigned to the family. If that didn't give her enough for the next morning's paper, a last minute check with Sergeant Grom would.

But the next day came earlier than Jennifer expected. Leo called shortly after 9:00 a.m.

'No, it's all right, Leo, I was just getting up — in an hour or two.'

'Sorry, but the big boss wants to see us in about an hour. Can you make it?'

'I dunno. How important is this guy to my career? Tell 'im I'm still in bed.'

'I like your sense of humour.'

'See you in forty-five, Leo. What's he want, anyway? You know?'

'Yeah, but I can't tell ya.'

'Wonderful. Should I think increase in salary or job-hunting?'

'Think anything you want; just get over here.'

'You print the sidebar, Leo?'

'Didn't change a word.'

'That mean you like it?'

'What do you think, Einstein?'

'Your kind of compliment. Thanks.'

Max Cooper's office was on the top floor of the *Day* building on Michigan Avenue. Even Leo appeared nervous.

'This is Jennifer Grey,' Leo said.

'Of course, sure,' the tall, thin, intense, distinguished publisher said. He had a reputation for looking good but being a little rough around the edges in personality. 'I shook hands with you at the Christmas party, didn't I?'

'No, I wasn't there. But I've seen you around, of course.'

'Of course, and I know your stuff. Sit down, sit down.'

Cooper joined Leo and Jennifer at a small wooden table and grinned at them. *If my career has just bitten the dust, he's pretty happy about it,* Jennifer decided.

'Let me get straight to the point, Miss Grey. I was serious about knowing your stuff. I read you every day, and I mean that. If you don't believe it, just quiz me.'

'I believe you.'

'Good, 'cause who knows how I'd do on a stupid quiz! Ha!'

Leo laughed. Jennifer smiled. Cooper continued.

'I, ah, was a police reporter myself when I started out. 'Course, my old man owned the whole chain, so I sorta had my pick, if you know what I mean.' Jennifer nodded. 'But anyway, I've always kept a close eye on the police beat.'

'Don't I know it?' Leo said.

'Yeah! You hear from me about that now and then, don't you, Lion? I call him Lion all the time, don't I, Lion?' Leo nodded. 'Well, Leo here was a police reporter way back too. Seems all the really good guys start there.'

Jennifer smiled at Max Cooper, enjoying whatever it was he was trying to say.

'Now me, before I went administrative, I went from the police beat to the sports page, then sports columnist and sports editor. I don't s'pose you've got any aspirations that way, do you, Miss Grey?'

'No, not really.'

'Well, 'course not. Not that a woman couldn't do a good job in sports. Wouldn't be against that at all if a qualified one wanted to or whatever, right? But you don't want that.'

'No, sir.'

'Well, I said I was going to get straight to the point, didn't I? I've been following your stuff for some time, and I've seen a spark there. I've seen attention to detail. I've seen a sensitivity there. I've seen the colour, the depth, the care — the types of things that most people wouldn't think an old hack like me would notice if they stared him in the face.'

'Thank you, sir.'

'Well, thank *you*. I mean, let's put the credit where the credit's due. Anyway, I've been pushing on the Lion here to get you into a little more feature stuff, not tryin' to tell him his job or anything, but just to see what your potential is. 'Course Leo agrees with me anyway; fact is, he saw you were special long before I did and told me so. You've got an ally there, Miss Grey.'

Jennifer smiled at Leo and refrained from telling Cooper that she was actually a *Mrs.*, as she usually did.

'Well, anyway, I didn't know what Leo had done this morning when I saw your sidebar on the little girl's murder. I mean, I wanted him to broaden your horizons a little, and you may have sensed he's been doing that, but letting you go and get so personal and opinionated and, uh, uh, earthy there — why, I just didn't know what to expect.'

'How did you feel about it, Mr. Cooper?' Jennifer asked.

'Me? Well, there wasn't anything wrong with your position as far as I'm concerned. I mean, I s'pose it's the type of thing I would have had no problem with on the editorial page or in some signed column or something. You were speaking my mind there, Miss Grey, and everybody's I assume, except for some misguided do-gooders who think more of the criminal than of the victim.'

'So, you don't feel it should have been placed next to the end of the story on page three?'

'I'm not saying that. I'm saying that I didn't know what to think when I saw it. I was moved by it, I must tell you that. I cried reading it, and I don't cry reading anything! The last time a newspaper piece moved me to tears was when Bob Greene did that thing in the *Trib* last year directed to the Tylenol killer. But I also must tell you that as soon as I got myself under control again, I was wearing my publisher's hat, and I started to worry. And I wanted to know why Leo had had you do it. I wasn't going to blame you. I was going to have the Lion's hide here if the phones started ringin' off the wall from the American Civil Liberties Union or who knows who else.'

Jennifer was puzzled. What exactly was the man trying to say?

'I know what you're thinking, Miss Grey. I know you're thinking that it's awful small of me to decide who gets called on the carpet and who doesn't, based on what the readers think of what goes in the paper. And you're right. But it's the name of the game. If they like it, I'm happy. If enough of 'em don't like it, then we've got trouble, whether I agree with the article or not. Which, as I already told you, I do.

'You see, we're still the third paper in a town with three papers, and I gotta tell ya, we're not ignoring the *Defender*, which a lot of people don't think qualifies as one of the biggies. It's comin' on, and we may be a town with four major papers again one day.

'But we thought Chicago could use another daily, even when the *Today* and the *Daily News* couldn't compete. Everybody knows we've succeeded, and we've hurt the competition — at least we've taken some of their

readers and advertisers. Personally, I think
competition can only help a paper, unless it
runs it out of business. And we have no inten-
tion of doing that.

'So, as tough and honest and real as I want
our paper to be, we still have to be a little
conservative in our policies so we don't lose
big batches of readers at a time. One or two
over a mistake or disagreement once in a while,
OK. But not hundreds of readers at a crack.
Can't afford it.'

'And is that what's happening this morning,
Mr. Cooper?'

The big boss squinted at her and then at Leo
Stanton. He rose and smiled. 'No, ma'am.
Apparently you haven't been listening to the
radio, watching the news, noticing the newspaper stands. Our pressrun ran out, Miss Grey.
It *ran out!* Do you know the last time a daily
paper in this town had to go back to press with
the same edition, Miss Grey? Neither do I. You
struck a nerve, lady. You hit big. You're the
talk of the town. People want today's issue of
the *Day*. And you know what that means? That
means they're going to want tomorrow's, and
the next day's, and the next — as long as there's
a personal column by you in there.'

Suddenly the man fell silent and sat again.
Jennifer took it as her cue to rise. Both Cooper
and Stanton were content to let her be the next
to speak. They looked at each other and
smiled. But she was troubled.

'Can I ask a question?' she said.

'Absolutely,' Cooper said.

'What would I be hearing right now if the reaction had been the opposite?'

'Good question, young lady. And I want to be honest with you. You see, you and I think a lot alike; I could tell that from your previous work, but especially in your column this morning. I like you; I like what you say. But if the public reaction had been negative, you wouldn't be standing here right now. Stanton would have been in trouble, and you would have been put out to pasture somewhere until this thing blew over.'

'If you don't mind my saying so, that sounds like a pretty shaky way to start a relationship as a columnist. Right or wrong, the public decides, correct?'

'It's a business, Miss Grey.'

'*Mrs.* Grey.'

'Excuse me.'

'That's all right. So if I become a daily columnist and the public suddenly decides it doesn't like me, I'm through?'

'I know how that sounds, Miss, ah, Mrs. Grey.'

'But that's the case.'

'Yes, that's the case.'

'I'll have to think about it.'

'Columnists don't get Guild rates, Mrs. Grey. We pay them like executives. For you, that would mean nearly a 50 per cent increase in pay.'

'Because of one emotional column?'

'Of course not. I told you, I've been reading you.'

'But the public reaction tipped the scales.'

'That's right,' Cooper said, suddenly sobering. 'Listen, sit down and let me tell you something, Mrs. Grey. If Leo hadn't told me a little about you, you can understand how I could be a little offended by your reaction here.'

'Yes, sir, I know, but it's just that —'

'I know. I know you're not motivated by money or power or prestige.'

'I'm not above being flattered by all that, but —'

'I know you're a religious person and that —'

'I prefer not to refer to my faith as religion.'

'Whatever, I know you're a churchgoing person and honest and all that.'

'And that would have to come through in any column I would write. Not in *every* column, but if you want my personality on paper, that would have to be a factor.'

Cooper furrowed his brow. 'It wasn't overt in the column this morning.'

'No, but I did pray about writing that.'

'Well, listen. If the public goes for it, you can write sermons for all I care. I'm not a man without principles myself, but I need a columnist the people want to read, and right now they want to read you, so you're it. It's yours if you want it. I'll have Leo put you on the bottom of page one, just like Keegan in the *Trib.* You can write what you want, but I assume you'd stay on this Heather Lauren case until it's resolved.'

'You may find that that's what got everyone so excited today. Not *me,* but the case itself.'

'Well, you may be right. I don't think so, but who knows? If you're right, the public will let us know, and you'll be back on the police beat.'

'Just like that?'

'Just like that. And let me ask you something. Where do you think Greene or Deeb or even Royko would be if the public suddenly decided they weren't worth the price of the paper every day?'

Jennifer blinked. 'But they don't write what the public wants to hear just to keep their jobs.'

'And we wouldn't want you to do that either. Just be yourself. As long as they love you, we'll have a tough time keeping you from jumping to one of the other papers.'

'Can I think about it?'

'For how long?'

'Twenty-four hours?'

'On one condition. You do at least one more piece like today's for tomorrow morning's paper.'

'I'm not sure I've got anything more to say like that.'

'It doesn't have to be just like it. Do your usual digging on the story today, write a straight piece, and then do a reflective sidebar. Where is your head since you wrote the last one and turned up more evidence? That type of thing is what the readers want to know.'

'I'll try,' Jennifer said.

Leo clapped. 'That's what she said last night, Max. Just before she wrote the winner.'

4 Jennifer's mind was jumbled as she swung off Bilford Boulevard onto the long and depressing Stivers Avenue. Just to drink in the atmosphere, she started four blocks from Lake Michigan and drove through more than eight miles of traffic-lights, crowded intersections, and elevated train underpasses from West Stivers.

She would have to have a talk with Leo. She had to smile at old man Cooper calling him Lion. Not Leo the Lion. Not The Lion. Just Lion. For how long had Leo been setting her up for this column possibility?

Already she'd heard on the radio that she wasn't exactly the hit of the *entire* town as Max Cooper had hoped. Indeed, the American Civil Liberties Union had released a statement demanding a retraction or an apology or a modification from her.

And there were rumours that another columnist, on her own paper, would be taking issue
with her in the next edition. She wondered
how Cooper would react to that. And what if
Cooper was right, that *she* had hit the nerve,
and thus her counterpart would be taking an
unpopular stand? Would that mean a sudden
end of his stint as a columnist?

The ACLU thing had initiated a mini-barrage
of callers telling a radio talk show host that
they agreed she'd been wrong. If she hadn't
been bolstered by the reactions of so many
others, including her boss and his boss, she
might have panicked, wondered if she had
done the right thing, looked for a way out.

But she didn't even have to ask to see again
the photo Martin Grom had showed her in the
West Side Precinct station house the day
before. She could remember. Would she ever
be able to forget?

Jennifer had a 1:00 p.m. appointment with
Angela Liachi, Heather Lauren's preschool
supervisor. But with a little time to spare, she
made a quick decision. She was going to drop
in on Heather's mother and, she hoped, Wyatt
Oliver.

She was ten minutes finding a parking place
on the street, and then she wasn't confident her
locked car was any more secure than if she had
left the keys in it.

As she headed toward 4326, she heard the
whistles and catcalls of groups of men she'd
seen huddled around burning refuse bins,

bouncing on their toes, hands jammed in their pockets except when lighting cigarettes.

Such groups dotted all of Stivers Avenue from just west of the Loop all the way through the high-rise projects and into the low-rise area. Now she was into the rows of three-storey, full-basement apartments that teemed with occupants, usually more than one family per apartment, at least two apartments per floor.

Jennifer fingered a can of chemical spray in her right coat pocket. Her bag strap was wrapped around her left arm. In her left hand she clutched her key ring, which contained a police whistle and a tiny razor blade that could be exposed with one snap of the wrist.

She could blind one, slice one, and scare a few with the whistle, but she didn't want to have to. She never had before, and now she simply wished she'd dressed in a less bourgeois style. What was it Jim had advised, besides all the artillery? 'Walk as if you know where you're going, as if you're expected any second, and as if you just might be a cop.'

More important, she thought, *is to actually know, and to actually be expected, and to actually be a cop.* Except for knowing where she was going, she had two strikes. If she didn't get an answer at the Oliver-Lauren residence, it was a good walk back to the car with at least one group of bored, unemployed men between it and her.

When she stole a glance back at them, however, it was apparent they had already given up on her. Now she noticed groups of preschool age children — some school age — frolicking near chain link fences in a world of grey and brown.

Jennifer looked at her watch. Almost twelve-thirty. Not much time. But then she probably wouldn't need much.

She sensed the eyes of many neighbours as she approached the front door of the dingy three-floor apartment building. The sign at the front read, 'Use Side Entrance.' She didn't like the looks of the dark space between buildings that led to the side door.

What was left of a crumbling path echoed under her boots as she moved around the building. The wind picked up momentum in the small passageway, hidden from the sun. She gritted her teeth at the bone-chilling gusts.

Jennifer sensed no movement from inside the building, though she knew someone had to be at home in at least one of the apartments. She was about to revert back to Plan A and drive the few blocks to locate Angela Liachi when she was startled by the rattle-crashing bursting open of the side door.

A tiny, sandy-haired boy, the size of a four-or five-year-old ran past her. 'Are you Elliott?' she called after him.

He nodded once as he ran, not looking back. He accelerated and turned a corner out of her sight. 'Is your mother at home?' she called again, but suddenly the entire neighbourhood was silent. Even the wind seemed to have stopped. It was as if no one could believe she had come there in her smart ensemble with her camel coat and her leather boots and her cover-girl makeup and her shining hair and then had the audacity to ask for someone.

Her eyes darted out from the darkness into the harsh sunlight that lit but didn't warm the street. The men were turning back to their oil drum fire. The kids stared at her from across the street. She waited until they lost interest and turned back to their games. Then she knocked on the warped wood of the side door.

She felt conspicuous. Watched. Unwanted.

She knocked again, more loudly. The firm tap of her knuckles pushed the door all the way open. Stunned, she stepped back and waited. Nothing.

Looking around one more time, Jennifer stepped inside and carefully shut the door behind her, feeling foolish. To her left, the stairs led to the cellar. To the right was an open archway into the kitchen of one of the ground floor flats. Straight ahead, the stairs led up. Heather Lauren's family lived on the first floor.

It seemed to her to take ages to make up her mind. She decided that Sergeant Martin Grom would soon convince a judge that he had enough on Wyatt Oliver and Cornelia Lauren to hold them and maybe even charge them with child abuse, manslaughter, murder, or whatever he wanted. She would then be unable to interview them.

She poked her head into the kitchen on the ground floor. 'Anyone at home?' she called quietly.

No response, even though she smelled food cooking.

She headed upstairs, holding her breath, listening for any sound of life. She knocked at a door, but footsteps on the second floor, resounding through the ceiling, scared her off. She hurried back down to the ground floor and waited by the side door again.

There was no sound of steps on the stairs, so she crept down to the cellar. The musty dampness, combined with the stench of a makeshift lavatory which drunks apparently used before staggering into their apartments at night, nauseated her.

She located an area surrounding a simple metal pole that had been roped off by the police. There was no sign of a struggle or of blood, but a blunted chalk tracing around the base of the pole marked where Cornelia Lauren told police she had found the tied, slumped body of her daughter.

Jennifer felt the bile rise in her throat and the anger shorten her breath. Why wouldn't someone have heard the girl's cries? Where were the ground-floor families when this happened? Where were they now?

She pressed her lips tight and hunched her shoulders against the chill, walking as close to the police rope as she could and peering into the shadows to try to imagine the scene. The memory of the horrible photo flooded her mind and she realized for the first time that it had been taken before the little body had been cut free.

Dear God, she prayed silently, fighting tears, *here's one I'll never understand. If it had to happen for some reason, at least help us find who did it.*

The sound of footsteps on the stairs above her froze Jennifer to her spot. Through the back of the stairs she could see bare feet and what appeared to be old, charcoal-coloured suit trousers. There was no exit except those stairs and nowhere to hide either.

Was he coming down to see if someone was there? Or because he knew someone was there? Or for a reason totally unrelated? The time for ducking behind something was past. She stood her ground and squinted at the small, muscley figure that had stopped at the bottom of the steps.

He glared at her without a word. He was not armed. His fingers were entwined in those second-hand suit trousers, holding them up for want of a belt. He wore a ribbed, sleeveless undershirt.

The light from the basement window shone on the back of his head, leaving his face dark, so Jennifer moved to her right to get a better look. His hair was long, greasy, and unkempt. He was unshaven. His eyes looked black. His muscles were taut.

Jennifer imagined she could smell him from ten feet away. She decided not to speak first. He spread his feet apart, as if ready to defend his position.

He looked Italian; he spoke truck driver with what Jennifer guessed was a CB-trained phony

Southern accent. 'The las' female found in this cellar was dead,' he said.

'I don't intend to be found here,' she said, surprising herself.

'Don't be too sure.'

She switched to the offensive, trying to sound friendlier. 'I, uh, was looking for the Lauren family. Mr. Oliver. Mrs. Lauren. Their son.'

'Down here you was lookin' for 'em?'

'Upstairs too. I didn't see anyone.'

'You knock?'

'Yes, sir.'

'I don't answer the door, an' my wife is in mournin'.'

'Are you also?'

'Ma'am?'

'Are you also in mourning, Mr. Oliver?'

'You want trouble, lady?' He swore. 'Who are you anyway?'

'Jennifer Grey. I write for the *Chicago Day* newspaper. Are you familiar with it?'

'I can't afford no newspaper. We ain't even paid off the TV yet.'

'Did you beat your wife's daughter, Mr. Oliver?'

His eyes narrowed. 'I think you better get your little self outta my house.'

'Is this your building?'

'I live here.'

'You own this basement?'

'Don't make me throw you out, writer lady.'

'Unless you have a weapon, you'll not be throwing me anywhere,' Jennifer said, her heart smashing against her ribs. 'Or are you going to tie me to a post and burn me and punch me?'

His hand shook. 'Are *you* armed, lady?'

'Yes, sir.'

He eyed her warily, then spoke softly. 'I'm bettin' you're lying,' and he moved quickly toward her.

Jennifer yanked both hands from her pockets simultaneously, flicking open the razor blade in her left hand, chemical spray poised in her right. Wyatt Oliver instinctively raised his hands in surrender, but he grabbed at his waistband again as his trousers started to fall. And Jennifer dashed past him, up the stairs, out the door, down the block, and, trembling as she fumbled with her keys, slid into her car. She didn't dare even look back as she sped toward the Park District centre.

She pulled into the parking area a few minutes ahead of schedule and dropped her head to the steering wheel, closing her eyes and trying to calm herself. *If that was my answered prayer, Lord,* she prayed wryly, *it could have waited.*

As she caught her breath, someone knocked on the window. Without thinking or looking up, she jammed the key back into the ignition and turned it on, throwing the car into reverse.

But as she whirled around to guide the car out of the car-park, she saw a short, dark-haired woman leap clear of the car, arms outstretched, terrified. Jennifer hit the brake and wound down her window with an embarrassed smile. 'Angela?'

'Miss Grey?' Angela said. 'What's got you so jumpy?'

'Not what. Who.'

'OK. Who?'

'Wyatt Oliver.'

'Why doesn't that surprise me?' Angela asked.

'Doesn't it?' Jennifer said. 'Tell me about it.'

'On one condition. You've got to get out from behind the wheel.'

5 Angela Liachi was attractive in a plump sort of way. Short. Dark. Intense. Fast-talking. New Yorkish. Her eyes shone as she smiled at Jennifer's jumpiness.

'Thought I was Wyatt Oliver, didja?'

Jennifer nodded.

'Let's take a walk. I don't wanna be anywhere near yer car, if you know what I mean.'

They walked three blocks north to the parking area of a boarded up former fast-food restaurant where they slowed and strolled around the building, turning their collars up against the wind. They ignored occasional honks and waves of passersby who thought they might be hookers.

'I saw your article today,' Angela said, stopping and facing the sun, squinting and enjoying the little heat she could drink from it.

Jennifer put a foot up on a cracked concrete carstop and studied the ground. 'Yeah? Kinda extreme, huh?'

'Are you kiddin'? If there was anything wrong with it, it was only that it was prob'ly too easy.'

Jennifer shot her a double take. 'Too easy? You ever try writing?'

'Nah, I don't mean the writing part of it. I mean taking the position. Too easy. Who could disagree?'

'The American Civil Liberties Union.'

Angela smiled a rueful smile and made an obscene gesture. 'Bleeding heart liberals.'

'People say social workers like you are bleeding heart liberal idealists,' Jennifer said.

'Oh, they do, huh? Well, I don't consider myself a social worker, a bleeding heart, or a liberal.'

'An idealist.'

'Dyed in the wool.'

The women smiled at each other.

'I have many questions for you about Heather Lauren —'

'And Wyatt Oliver, right?'

'Of course, if you know anything —'

'If I *know* anything! *I* could write you an article on Wyatt Oliver.'

'I was going to say that I had a lot of questions for you about the case, and I appreciate your agreeing to see me, but first I wanted to talk about you.'

That made Angela nervous. She started moving again, and Jennifer had to shift her weight quickly and get going to keep up. Angela swore. 'It's cold,' she added.

'It's nothing personal,' Jennifer said. 'I'm just curious.'

'And you're not gonna print anything in the paper about me, are you?'

'No. Well, I might quote you on the Heather Lauren case, that's all.'

'You can't quote everything I say about that. You wouldn't want to.'

'We'll get to it. First, just tell me —'

'I know what you're going to ask.'

'How do you know what I'm going to ask?' Jennifer was smiling, but becoming exasperated.

'Because I get it all the time. I gotta tell ya, I'm not good copy. Every few months, some well-dressed — nothing   personal — reporter from some magazine or newspaper or radio or TV station comes into my little ghetto here and asks me what motivates me. That's the big word. *Motivation.* Tell me the truth, is that what you were going to ask?'

'Yes.'

'Still want an answer?'

'I must have missed all those interviews you've done. I've never heard or read your answer.'

'That's because they never use it. I don't give 'em enough.'

'And if you did, you wouldn't let them print it or broadcast it, am I right?'

'That's not it, Mis, uh, Grey —'

'Call me Jennifer, please.'

'OK, Jennifer please,' she said, smiling. 'The point is that I don't have any grand story to tell. Why would a skilled, privileged, educated, established, unlimited-future-type like me come to the seediest part of Chicago and — they always put this in quotes — *give her life* to the blacks, Hispanics, and poor whites?'

'It's a good question, Angela. If all those reporters from all those different media ask it, it must be because they believe the public wants to know.'

'But Jennifer, it would be a good question only if there was a good answer. I'd love to be able to spin a yarn for you, tell you that despite my privileged upbringing, a chance encounter with a not-so-fortunate person taught me the meaning of selfless love. I can't. Didn't happen. I'm not a socialist. I'm not religious; I wasn't called here. I just heard about the opportunity, thought it fit me, and it seemed like the right thing to do at the time.'

'How long have you been here?'

'Eight years.'

'Eight years! That's got to be some kind of a record, doesn't it?'

'For one programme in one neighbourhood, it is. By almost double.'

'You're proud of that, I can tell.'

'Granted.'

'Why?'

'I don't know. I came here to do a job, and I'm doin' it. Does there have to be more than that? You see how unpublishable that is?'

'I'd publish it.'

'And break your promise?'

'No, I mean I would if you'd let me.'

'I won't.'

'I realized that. Does anything make you angry?'

'I'm pretty even, Jennifer. I've seen it all here. I've been disappointed at slow progress. I miss kids when I feel I've got somewhere with them and then the parents move them away in the middle of the night to stay a step ahead of their creditors.'

'Is this job dangerous?'

'Yeah, but I don't want to talk about that either. I live in the neighbourhood. I'm known. I use lots of locks on the door. I don't own a car. I don't go out alone at night. If I was mugged or my place invaded, I'd give whoever it was anything they wanted. I survive. I've got friends.'

'Do you arm yourself?'

'No, but I'll bet *you* do.'

'I do,' Jennifer admitted.

'Right again.'

'Are you bitter, cynical?'

'Some. Hard not to be here. Aren't you, after spending a little time here?'

'Yes. You know, Angela, I asked you what I wanted to ask you, but I feel like I haven't found out anything. You're not the typical visionary, but something must make you tick, keep you here, motivate you — sorry.'

'It's all right. I knew you'd get back to it. I love the kids. I don't know why. I honestly don't know why I love the kids. There was nothing in my background that pointed me this way. I was an only child. I studied literature at Alfred University. I had no degree in this kind of work, no training. I just applied. Not much competition, I can tell you that. We done with me?'

'I guess so, but you fascinate me.'

'That embarrasses me.'

'I wouldn't have guessed that anything embarrasses you.'

'I cover well. You've already got more out of me than anyone else ever did, and you promised not to use it. So let's stop wasting your time and talk about Heather Lauren.'

'I don't consider it a waste of my time, but I don't want to waste yours.'

'Talking about me wastes my time, but I'm not angry. I'm flattered. But I've also done enough of it.'

It hadn't been said unkindly, but Jennifer got the message. 'Why did you agree to talk to me about Heather?'

'Because Wyatt Oliver murdered her, and I'd like to see him fry for it.'

'You *know* he did it?'

'I'd lay odds.'

'Why?'

'The man is no good. I'm supposed to be used to his kind of people, but not everybody who has the misfortune to live around here is Wyatt Oliver's kind of person. His wife, for instance. She's limited.'

'Limited?' Jennifer asked, taking Angela by the arm and leading her around a corner of the boarded up building to get out of the direct wind.

'Psychologically. She makes me mad, but I can sympathize with her.'

'I'm sorry, I'm not following you.'

'The woman is scared to death of Oliver. She needs him, she thinks, but she brings in more money than he does, which isn't much. He terrorizes her and the children, and she won't lift a finger. The cops have been over a time or two. But when the woman won't press charges, they lose interest in responding to the neighbours' calls when they've finally had enough of the screaming. You wonder where the other tenants were when that precious child was murdered in the basement?'

Jennifer nodded, but Angela's voice had broken and her chin quivered, and she couldn't speak. Jennifer tried to give her time to recover. 'Yes, that's exactly what I thought when I was in the basement and saw where it had happened. It's an old rickety building, and the sound would carry. No one heard anything?'

'Have you asked them?' Angela managed. 'That's part of your job, isn't it?'

'I will be asking, if I dare go back there.'

Angela crossed her arms and raised her chin, closing her eyes, then opening them and lowering her gaze to Jennifer's. 'I want to tell you that I'm used to the kinds of things that go on around here. I know the frustration, the sense of emptiness, the futility. I know why women stay with men they shouldn't and why teenagers take drugs and pull robberies and why men come home drunk every night and can't keep jobs. I know why families scream at each other and fight and throw things.'

She was becoming emotional again, but this time Jennifer just let her regain her composure in her own time. Angela turned sideways to Jennifer and leaned a shoulder against the building.

'I understand why the cops have to cruise around the area and why they have to keep people from killing each other. But there's something I don't understand. I don't understand a woman, the real parent to her children, letting anyone lay a hand on them. Isolated instances, OK. Fits of rage, forgivable once in a great while. And I know a drunken lout, many times stronger than a woman, can intimidate her to the point where she feels powerless to help herself. But if he beat the kids one night, wouldn't you be hitting the road the next day, first chance you got?'

Jennifer nodded; she was moved. Angela fell silent, and Jennifer didn't know where to go from there. She had a feeling Angela hadn't finished, and she knew she'd have to ask again if Angela had any hard evidence against Wyatt Oliver.

In an uncharacteristic loss of concentration, Jennifer suddenly found herself wishing she didn't have to wait until Friday night to see Jim. She missed him. She wanted to talk to him about the column possibility. But they had limited themselves to Wednesdays and weekends.

She scolded herself for even thinking about

that now. Angela was staring into the distance. *Interesting woman,* Jennifer decided. *She gets emotional, but she doesn't lose control. She doesn't break down.*

'Elliott came to the preschool group first,' Angela said suddenly. 'They had moved in from the South somewhere, and he was supposed to be in kindergarten. I didn't ask any questions. He was a good kid, quiet, but often short of energy and hungry.

'We give the kids milk, and once a week we get day-old pastries from one of the local bakeries. All the kids love 'em, of course, but Elliott inhaled 'em. I mean, he'd eat five or six. Every time I turned around, he'd sneak another. At first I was afraid he'd get sick, but then I feared it was all he was getting to eat.'

'Not a very good diet,' Jennifer said.

'Better than nothing. So I started smuggling him fruit. Terribly small, thin child, but when he got some food in him, he loved to run.'

'He ran past me this morning.'

'Yeah? The old man is feeding him well since Heather's been gone. Keeping him quiet is my guess.'

'What makes you so sure about Oliver?'

'I've visited that place more than once. It's a hole, but I'm used to that. What I didn't like was that Wyatt Oliver didn't care that I was there; he treated his woman and her children the same as always. They waited on him hand and foot. They brought him beer and snacks, and he sat in front of a little colour TV that must have cost him a month's unemployment money.'

'He says he's still paying for it.'

'I'll bet he *is*. Probably stole it. Anyway, I suggested that Heather was old enough to come to the group and also that it would be a good idea to be sure they had a good lunch on pre-school days because we had so much activity. Mrs. Lauren appeared to understand, but Oliver was incensed. "You just make 'em behave there, and we'll make 'em behave here."

'I didn't know what that had to do with a good lunch, so I told him I'd never had a bit of trouble with Elliott and that I assumed I wouldn't with Heather either. He told me to just let him know if I did and I'd never have any more trouble.'

'Scary.'

'I should say. Scared me. I wanted to adopt both kids right then and there. Both so sweet. Heather started coming to the Monday-Wednesday-Friday group after that. I couldn't get her to say a word to anyone, not even "Hi". But she always came. Would sometimes laugh at the stories, always participated in games. But my first clue of what was happening in that home was when we had an outing at the Y.'

'A swimming party?'

'Right. A lot of the kids didn't even have suits, so they were provided by the Y. It was a bring-your-lunch and spend the day type of a thing. The Lauren kids didn't bring suits and wouldn't accept suits, either. That was the first time I heard Heather talk.

'I sat them down and told them how much fun they'd be missing, and I asked Elliott to tell me why they didn't want to swim. He looked past me as if he hadn't heard. I asked him again. He ignored me.

'I asked him again, and Heather piped up. "We got ouchies," she said, and Elliott leaped to his feet and screamed at her, "Don't tell! Don't tell! Don't tell! Don't tell!" '

6 By the time Jennifer left Angela Liachi a couple of hours later, she had heard the full story of Angela's encounters with Wyatt Oliver.

After that day at the Y, when Angela had been forced to let Elliott and Heather just sit and watch the others, because — she assumed — they had sores on their bodies where people couldn't see them, she called the Department of Social Services.

'I talked to the woman there I deal with a lot. Nathalie Benedict. She set up a bogus physical exam for my group one Friday, sort of swooped in, pulled each kid behind a screen, and had a doctor check their pulses, look down their throats, and put a stethoscope to their bare chests.

'The idea was that the doctor would be so quick and intimidating that he could just whip through the exam and at the end tug their shirts up for a quick listen. By then, Elliott wasn't coming any more. He'd started kindergarten.

'Little Heather, who hadn't spoken to me before or after the incident at the Y, kept looking at me fearfully as she stood in line, waiting for her turn with the doctor. Her huge, sad eyes begged me to rescue her, but I alternately ignored her or smiled at her to boost her courage.

'The woman from Social Services knew which one they were really after, and she played it just right. She just ushered Heather in and spoke softly and encouragingly to her, and when the time came to lift her little shirt, Heather flinched, but let the doctor do it.

'Heather came out tearful and scowled at me, as if I should have protected her from that indecency, but I didn't know if they'd found anything or what.'

'Did she make you feel guilty?'

'Hardly. The whole scheme was for her benefit. She couldn't know that, but I did it for her, and I wasn't going to feel bad about it. I was sorry she had to be embarrassed, but better embarrassed than killed in her own home.'

'Did they find anything?'

Angela had started walking back toward the centre. 'I knew when it was all over and they were putting their equipment away. The kids, for the most part, had loved it. No injections. Quick and painless. They'd been tickled. They asked questions. The doctor stayed and answered a few, but it was obvious to me that both the doctor and Nathalie were upset; it showed all over their faces. They were grim. Boiling. They waited in the parking area until the class was over and the kids went off home.'

'What had they found?'

Angela stopped and faced Jennifer. 'Sores. Burns. Burn scars.' She bit her lip and looked down. 'I was angry, so mad I was going to run after Heather and keep her from going home. Nathalie had to calm me down. She said I could cause more trouble by doing that right then. She said there was no way to immediately pull a child from her home and that if we tried, the parents would get her back and punish her worse for telling on them.

'I didn't care. I wanted to grab the kid and hide her somewhere. You had to have seen this girl, Jennifer, to know what I mean. So quiet, so sweet, so giving and loving and lovable. Short cropped blonde hair, skinny little arms and legs. Never wore dresses or skirts. Always jeans. Probably owned one pair.'

Jennifer put her hand on Angela's shoulder. 'You had enough talking for today?'

Angela shook her head. 'I want to finish this. I pushed Social Services to file a report and press charges, and I know they did, but it took so long that I took matters into my own hands.'

'Meaning?'

'I visited Heather's home again. When Elliott saw me, he headed for the hills.'

'Elliott?'

'Yup. He knew that whatever had started that day at the Y was coming to a head, and he didn't want to get punished for letting the cat out of the bag.'

'What did you do, Angela — just confront Oliver?'

'No, I wasn't daft enough to do that. Might as well have though; I didn't fool him. I said I wanted to talk about Heather's progress. He ignored me and just sat there watching his TV. Cornelia sat with me, looking fearful, as if she wanted me to finish and get going.

'I talked about general things, motor skills, Heather's shyness, that type of stuff. Then I said that it was apparent she'd been hurt somehow and that it hampered her during playtime. I just threw it out there without comment, hoping that her mother would at least try to explain it, even with a lie.'

'She didn't?'

'She shot a terrified glance at Oliver and fell silent. I mean silent. She hardly moved. I said, "Well, is she recovering from whatever happened, or would you like me to arrange for treatment? It'll be free." With that, Oliver wrenched around in his chair and swore at me.

'He said, "We can take care of our own here, and we don't need any charity. Just let the kid be. She's all right. Just stop babying her." '

'He was admitting she'd been hurt,' Jennifer said.

'I thought so, and it made me mad. Maybe he could see through my offer and caught the veiled threat that if something didn't stop in that household, I was going to city authorities. I knew I was about to say something I'd regret, so I forced myself to put it in the form of a question rather than an accusation.

'I said, "What happened to her anyway, Mr. Oliver? She looks as if she's had some sort of an accident that burned her." He stood quickly and kicked the TV switch off, sending the stand rocking and almost tipping the whole set over. I was frozen in my chair.

'He swore again and said, "How do you know what kinda sores she's got on her body? I never seen any sores on her." Now I was livid. I said, "Why don't you ask her mother or call her in here and see for yourself?" It was the first time I sensed any vulnerability in the man. He said, "She fell down the stairs about a month ago and she burned herself on the hot plate about a week later." '

'Did you believe him?'

'Would you have? Being burned on a hot plate is a mighty unusual injury, other than on a finger. Anyway, the Social Services doctor put in his report that many of the burns appeared to have been caused by cigarettes. I stood and moved toward the door. I thanked him for his time and left him with a not-so-veiled threat.

'I said, "I'd hate to have to report to Social Services that this is an unsafe home for a little girl." '

'He let you get away with saying that?'

'Not entirely. He said, "You're gonna find out that this ain't a safe place for you." And he started toward me. His wife cried out, and as I ran down the stairs I heard him laughing. By the time I reached the door on the ground floor, he was screaming at her.'

'I'm surprised he let Heather come to pre-school after that,' Jennifer said, 'now that the cat was out of the bag. These guys usually protect themselves.'

'She didn't come again for more than a month. I panicked. I asked her friends if she was still around, and they assured me she was. I walked through the neighbourhood several times, and occasionally I'd see her, but when she saw me, she'd run away. Finally I talked to Elliott.'

'Really? You hadn't talked to him for quite a while by then.'

'Right, but I ran into him at the park and asked him how he liked school. We probably talked more for those few minutes than we had all the time he'd been in preschool. It was so sweet. I asked him if there was anyone at school who sneaked him doughnuts and rolls, and he smiled so shyly and with such obvious gratefulness at the memory that it made my whole career here worthwhile.'

Angela invited Jennifer into the building and into her tiny, cluttered office where she made two cups of black coffee. 'I have to admit,' Jennifer said, 'even after all you've told me, I don't feel like I know those two kids.'

'That's just it,' Angela said. 'I never felt that way either. When kids don't express them-selves, you tend to assume characteristics based on how they look, how sweet they are, how shy they are. I'm sure I've got both Elliott and Heather idealized in my mind. To me, they were both precious children. Victimized. They had that look like you had, that look Oliver gives people.'

'That look?'

'Like they've just seen the devil himself.'

'He left you with that look twice, didn't he, Angela?'

'Three times.'

'Three?'

'I saw him once more. This is the good part. I threatened him.'

'Whoa, let me catch up a little!'

'Well, Heather started coming to preschool again; and she appeared healthy. There were no signs of any injuries. She was running and playing and talking with the other kids. Things were fine for probably six months.'

'That long?'

'I'm not saying she wasn't still being abused. I'm sure she was. But the man was being careful. I mean, he'd always been careful enough to keep from hurting her where it would show. But I noticed no tentativeness, no physical tenderness, and she finally even started talking to me.'

'Really?'

'Nothing big. Just greetings and questions. Very shyly, very quietly. I tried desperately to build a relationship with her so she would tell me the next time she got hurt. That was a pipe dream, but I tried.'

'And did she?'

'Tell me, you mean? No. I found out about

the next incident through Nathalie at Social Services. They got a call from the casualty department at St. Anthony's. The mother had brought Heather in during the middle of the night with an unbelievable injury.'

Angela stopped talking. Jennifer waited. Angela straightened papers on her desk and stacked some books on the shelf. When she finally spoke again, her voice was thick. 'Jennifer,' she said, 'if you want a crusade, a campaign, an issue, it's the red tape in this city! We're choking on it!'

Jennifer didn't understand, but she wasn't going to interrupt Angela now that her anger was boiling over. She had apparently been so crushed by the death of Heather Lauren that she had been unable to fully express it. If it was coming out this way, that was fine. It would be good for her.

'It's not Social Services' fault. They have no more power than the Park District does. All they can do is file reports and make recommendations. I think they should have recommended Heather and Elliott's removal from that home after the first physical exam, but they advised observation instead.

'But when they got the report from St. Anthony's, they moved quickly. As far as I know, the paperwork is still floating through city hall somewhere.'

'Can you tell me about the injury?'

'The girl was nearly dead, Jennifer! They had to perform artificial resuscitation on her twice!'

'What had happened to her?'

'She was in shock. She could have died from the shock. Shock is probably what really killed her a few days ago.'

'The autopsy will show that. But why was she in shock that first time?'

'Lots of bruises and burns, but a horrible injury to her seat.' Again Angela was too upset to talk, but Jennifer wanted to hear it all.

'To her seat?'

'Oh, Jennifer,' Angela whispered, 'Nathalie showed me a picture that I can't erase from my mind.' And she cried.

'I saw one of those recently too.'

'You saw that picture?'

'I saw the one taken by the police in the cellar where she was found.'

'I don't want to see that one. The hospital photo was all I ever care to see.'

'Can you tell me about it?'

Angela walked to the window and stared out across the parking area. The sun was now hidden, and the day had turned grey. 'The skin was burned black, and the only thing recognizable was the brand name of the hot plate, which had been seared into her in reverse. Someone had sat her on that hot plate!'

'What was the mother's story?'

'She just wanted them to hurry, because she said her husband, whom she listed as Wyatt Lauren, had forbidden her to bring the girl in, but he was sleeping and she needed to get treatment and hurry back. The hospital wanted to admit Heather, but her mother refused. That's when they called the police.'

'The police were involved in this before? I didn't even know that.'

'You didn't know that the West Side homicide sergeant wanted the kids out of there but couldn't get the clearance?'

'No, but I'll be asking him about that today. What did Mrs. Lauren tell the police?'

'Her story was that Heather had sleep-walked, fallen down the stairs, landed on the hot plate, and passed out from the pain or from hitting her head or something. They asked why her husband had not wanted her brought in for treatment, and she said he didn't have money or insurance and thought they could take care of her themselves.'

'And the police believed her?'

'No. In fact, Wyatt Oliver was held overnight for questioning.'

'I wonder why none of the media are aware of that,' Jennifer said. 'You're sure of this?'

'That's what Social Services told me when I screamed at them about getting the kids out of that house. They said they'd done everything they could think of. *I* could think of something else.'

'Such as.'

'If you can't separate the children from the parents, you have to separate the parents from the children.'

'How do you do that?'

'When Wyatt Oliver was released and I realized the full import of what was going on —'

'Meaning?'

'Meaning that the man had apparently

almost killed the girl and was now back in the same home situation. I stewed for a day, then walked through the neighbourhood. Heather was outside, watching the other kids play. Elliott was very attentive to her, checking with her every few minutes.

'She was pale, cold, stiff. When she walked, she hardly bent her knees. It was pitiful. I stormed to her apartment building and charged up the stairs. I surprised the life out of Wyatt Oliver.

'I banged on the door so loudly that they didn't want to answer. I said, "I know you're in there, you lazy thing! Answer the door!" His wife opened the door, and he stood behind her with a small stick in his hand.

' "You gonna use that on me?" I asked him, "or do you only beat up little girls?" His wife hid her face in her hands and started to move away, and he acted like he was going to come at me. I wish he had. I'd have killed him.'

'Do you really think you would have?'

'I know I would have. He's a strong guy, but I was so furious I could have torn him in two with my bare hands. He saw it in my eyes, Jennifer, because he was scared to come closer. I said, "Come here, you slime," and he tried to slam the door on me. I put my foot in it and took a good bruise to the ankle, but not before I promised to make him pay with his life.'

'You really did?'

'You bet. I said, "If one more thing happens to those kids, Oliver, I'll kill you." '

7

'I'm glad, for your sake, that you didn't fulfil your promise, Angela.'

'There's still time.'

'Don't say that.'

'I read your column, Jennifer. Don't tell me you and a lot of other people wouldn't love to do it for me.'

'I wouldn't.'

'Then your column was a lie?'

'I didn't say in my column that *I* wanted to mete justice out to the murderer.'

'Oh, I see. You want him to die for the crime, but you wouldn't want *your* pretty hands soiled in the process.'

'Angela, you're upset. You know what I mean, and I know what you mean. And I have to believe that you don't seriously intend to do harm to a person you can't even be sure is guilty.'

'I'm sure. Are you saying you're not?'

'How could I know?'

'You know. Don't you know? You had an encounter with the murderer today, didn't you?'

'How could I know he was the murderer, Angela?'

'Will you get off this Pollyanna kick? You look into your heart of hearts and tell me you've got one shred of doubt whether that scoundrel murdered his own daughter.'

Jennifer couldn't speak.

'One shred,' Angela challenged again.

Jennifer stared at her.

'All right,' Angela said, 'so get off your high horse.'

'But Angela, you're a mature adult. You know you can't throw your life and career away by actually killing a man.'

'I know what you're saying, Jennifer, but I'm so tired of the bureaucracy, the stalling, the time-wasting. Who needs this? Society lets this man get away with everything short of murder, and now it appears he's going to get away with *that!*'

'He won't get away with it.'

'Not if I have anything to do with it, he won't.'

'What would you do, Angela, if he really did slip through somehow? If through further investigation, they couldn't find enough evidence to convict him?'

Angela Liachi sat heavily across from Jennifer and looked deep into her eyes. 'If it happened today?' she said. 'If I learned it today and I saw him today and I had the opportunity, I fear I would kill the man. And I mean that.'

'Do you want me to protect you from yourself?' Jennifer offered.

'What do you mean?'

'You want to take a few days off and cool down, come and stay with me for a while? You sound serious.'

'I *am* serious. You think I'd like that, don't you? You think I'd welcome the chance to get out of this rat hole, start thinking like a rational human being, and enjoy the comforts of your Uptown place.'

'It isn't that.'

'It isn't? Then what is it? You want me for column material? You promised not to write about my motivation for working here, but you didn't promise you wouldn't write about my motivation for murder. Am I gonna read about this in the paper tomorrow morning?'

'Of course not.'

Apparently Angela believed her, because she finally broke down and sobbed. 'I appreciate you,' she admitted through her tears. 'And I'm sorry I said that. I've known you only a little while, but I can tell you wouldn't use me.'

'And the little I've known *you,*' Jennifer said, 'tells me you really don't want to end your career by committing a murder.'

Angela's shoulders heaved. She shook her head. 'I don't really,' she said. 'I'm like you; I want someone else to do it. It scares me though. I really think I'd do it if I saw the man today.'

Jennifer stood and made more coffee. Angela appeared surprised that Jennifer would feel free to do that. She thanked her and asked, 'Want something on-the-record that even the cops don't know yet?'

Jennifer was almost too shocked to respond. 'Are you serious?'

'Sure. Get out your pad. You remember Mrs. Lauren told the cops that Heather didn't come home from preschool? And that she didn't report her missing or tell anyone else outside the family until she found her in the basement two days later? Well, Heather hadn't been to preschool for weeks, and she definitely wasn't there Monday.'

'I don't get it.'

'Neither do I.'

'The police didn't come asking?'

'No, and they should have, shouldn't they?'

'Of course.'

'I'd been asking around about Heather. The kids said she was still in the neighbourhood but that she couldn't come to preschool. I thought maybe she was being abused again, and I walked through the neighbourhood a few times, but I always missed her. Either that or she avoided me.'

'Likely?'

'Under threat of her father, if you can call him that? Sure.'

'So you really hadn't seen her for a long time?'

'Not since right after she'd been treated for the hot plate burns.'

'Why didn't you come forward when you saw the misinformation in the paper?'

'I just have,' Angela said.

'And I can quote you on this?'

'That's what I said.'

'Thanks for everything, Angela. And do me a favour, will you? Don't do anything rash, regardless of what happens with Wyatt Oliver.'

Angela forced a smile, but said nothing.

Not a half hour later, Jennifer was waiting to see Nathalie Benedict at the West Side Social Services Centre. The receptionist kept relaying questions from the inner office. 'You won't need much time? You'll accept no-comment reactions when Mrs. Benedict feels they're necessary? She can be off-the-record when she requests it?'

Jennifer agreed to everything. Finally, she was ushered in. Nathalie Benedict was a tall, pleasant, healthy-looking, almost handsome woman — classy, but past her prime. In her mid-fifties, she still carried the evidence of an early season tan, aided by heavy makeup, styled hair, lots of jewellery, and expensive clothes. Her nails were long and painted lavender to go with her layered outfit.

'You're covering the Lauren case?' she asked.

'Yes, ma'am, thank you for seeing me. I wonder if you can tell me about the time you had

Heather Lauren examined by a Social Services doctor.'

Mrs. Benedict grew cold and stared at her. 'When I what?'

'When you took a doctor into the West Side Park District preschool at the request of the teacher and staged a bogus class physical so the doctor could get a look at what Heather Lauren had told the teacher were "ouchies".'

Mrs. Benedict lit a cigarette and squinted as she took a deep drag and, instead of blowing the smoke away, merely opened her mouth and let it curl up in a thick column. 'I have no comment about that,' she said evenly.

'Are you saying it didn't happen?'

'I'm saying I prefer not to comment about it.'

'Did you yourself see the injuries on Heather Lauren's body?'

'No,' she said, and quickly realizing the implication of that, added, 'comment'.

'No? Or no comment?'

'No comment.'

'Can you tell me about the injury to Heather Lauren that your office was made aware of several weeks ago when she was taken to St. Anthony's casualty department in the middle of the night with third-degree burns to the buttocks?'

'We were made aware of that, yes.'

'And did you make a recommendation based on that?'

'Our recommendations to the police and other agencies are matters of public record.'

'Then you won't mind telling me what that was?'

'Our recommendations? I don't remember. You may feel free to look it up at city hall.'

'Did you not recommend that both Heather Lauren and her older brother, Elliott, be removed from their home?'

'I don't recall.'

'Does it not sound logical?'

'Without studying the documents, I couldn't comment —'

'Are you saying there's a possibility that you *didn't* recommend that a child be removed from a home where such injuries had been inflicted?'

Mrs. Benedict had not appreciated being interrupted, and while it was not Jennifer's usual style, she sensed there wasn't a lot of time on this case. Wyatt Oliver either had to be indicted or exonerated, and she was beginning to share Angela Liachi's frustration over the red tape.

'I will talk with you off-the-record,' Mrs. Benedict said suddenly, surprising Jennifer. 'Do I have your word?'

'Yes, ma'am.' But Nathalie didn't start talking until Jennifer returned her notebook to her bag.

'I know you have been talking to Miss Liachi, because you couldn't have known of the physicals otherwise. And I want you to know I share her anger and misery over this death. But I also want to make clear that I need my job, I want my job, and I have never made a practice of bad-mouthing my agency or the police or the courts.'

'I understand. Is there something you would tell me off-the-record about them, however?'

'I must have your word.'

'Absolutely confidential.'

'My prediction is that this Oliver will never come to trial. They so seldom do. It was obvious from the way Cornelia Lauren acted that night in the hospital that he had abused the child and also that the whole family was terrified of him. She would not budge from the crazy sleepwalking story, and she has never pressed charges against the man for any reason.

'Strange as it may seem, as many times as our agency has been in that home and been aware of the abuse, and as many times as Angela Liachi has taken it upon herself to do our work — and I don't blame her for a little zeal — the man has never been charged with one crime similar to what was committed this week.'

'Nothing? No public disturbance, family quarrel, anything?'

'The only thing on his record, and the police will bear this out, is some public drunkenness. We have recommendations in, yes. I would like to see the kids, well, the boy now, removed from that environment. But someone had better get something on that quote/unquote father, or Elliott will grow up right where he is. If Oliver doesn't kill him, too.'

'You know these people, don't you? I mean,

you know their names as if you're familiar with the case.'

Mrs. Benedict nodded. 'All I can give you on-the-record is that we are aware of the case, we hope the guilty party will be found, and that our previous recommendations regarding the disposition of the family are on public record.'

'That's it?'

'That's it. I wish I could be of more help.'

'Off-the-record again, then. What are the answers for cases like this? What can anyone do to speed things along, to get action, to protect children from such an environment?'

'Besides killing the abusive parent you mean? I wish I knew.'

'I wish you hadn't said that.'

'You *have* been talking to my friend, Angela, haven't you?'

'Uh-huh.'

'Don't worry about her. She blows off a lot of steam, and she's usually right, too. But she's not going to do anything more to Wyatt Oliver than yell and scream at him like she did once.'

'She's not serious about wanting to kill him?'

'Oh, she's serious enough. I just don't think she would or could if she wanted to. Anyway,' she concluded with a weary sigh, 'if she really wants to, she'd better take a number and get in line.'

8 Jennifer had a few hard questions for Sergeant Martin Grom at the West Side Precinct station. But he wasn't there when she arrived. That surprised her. He knew she was coming.

As she waited in the lobby and idly read the plaques and citations and Police Youth League trophies, she smiled at the memory of her first encounter with the man the officers called The Lug.

Grom was a big redhead, about six feet three inches and broad in a soft sort of way that wasn't flabby, but was miles from being in shape. He walked with his elbows away from his body, swinging his arms like a robot. People tended to stay out of his way.

He was gruff and blunt, but he waxed fatherly in the presence of the opposite sex. Jennifer's Jim had always got a kick out of

Martin, and he seemed to have a decent reputation in the department. He often brought his kids in on his days off. Couldn't stay away, but had to babysit. He had a bunch of 'em, but all were boys except his five-year-old.

'Your daughter's name again?' Jennifer asked when The Lug finally arrived and waved her into his office.

'Jackie,' he said, not beaming as usual. 'We call her Red.'

'Everyone in your family have a nickname?'

'No, she's the only one.'

Jennifer smiled, assuming no one called Grom The Lug to his face. 'I don't think I've ever seen you in uniform before, Martin. You still in homicide?'

'Oh, yeah. I wear it now and then. Special occasions and so forth.'

'This is a special occasion?'

'Nah.' But he didn't appear eager to elaborate.

'Martin, can I ask you some questions?'

'I thought that's why you were here,' he said. 'Fire away, but let's make it fast.'

That wasn't like him either. She studied him for a moment, but he wouldn't return her gaze. 'Why didn't you tell me Heather Lauren had been burned before?'

'What're you talking about?'

'I'm talking about St. Anthony's, the middle of the night, third-degree burns with a hot plate, holding Oliver for questioning.'

'Ah, that *was* Oliver, wasn't it?'

'Oh, I get it. You didn't remember till just now.'

'That's right.'

'That's ridiculous. A man of your ability, your concentration, your attention to detail?'

'So what? What do you want from me, Jenn? OK, we tried to book the guy the first time around —'

'But that *wasn't* the first time around, Martin. Social Services wanted you to look into the family when they discovered injuries on the girl's body in a physical exam.'

'Oh, yeah? You're onto everything, huh? Well, did whoever tell you that also tell you what kinda heat Social Services got for that little sham or how the fur would have flown if we'd used that little bit of information on this Oliver creep?'

'What are you saying?'

'You tell me, you know so much.'

'Martin, don't be mean with me.'

'I'm sorry, Jenn, but this girl has been dead probably since Monday, discovered only yesterday, and already I'm getting pressure to arrest somebody.'

'Pressure from whom?'

'What'dya mean from whom? From downtown, from the papers, from everybody. From you.'

'Did I say anything like that?'

'Come on, Jennifer! You sit here all but askin' me why I don't have Wyatt Oliver locked up. You think I don't get your drift?'

'I wasn't driving at that, Martin.'

'Then what *were* you driving at?'

'I just want to know why there has been so much activity concerning the man, admittedly with no convictions, but without the press knowing anything about it?'

'We don't have to tell you anything you don't ask.'

'But you have in the past, and I've appreciated it.'

'I haven't given you much.'

'That's the most accurate thing you've said so far.' He looked pained, but she plunged ahead. 'Tell me what kind of trouble Social Services would have been in if you'd used the evidence they turned up in the class physicals.'

Grom stood and rested an elbow on a bookshelf next to his desk. He sighed. 'Awright, you can't give physicals without parental consent. All we needed to do was use that information and it would have come out that they'd pulled a bogus deal. Other parents with kids in that class would've demanded to know if their children had been examined in that scheme, and then the whole city would have come down on our heads. The evidence would have been inadmissible.'

'So you had to forget it, even when she turned up terribly burned at St. Anthony's several months later?'

'We put a lot of heat on the man, Jennifer. Hank Henry and I handled the interrogation, and I'd like to think we had the guy on the ropes. But the woman wouldn't point the finger at him. The little girl wasn't talking. The neighbours heard only screaming and crying and an argument about taking her to the hospital. Oliver didn't give Cornelia Lauren permission to take Heather to the hospital, so she had to wait until she could get him dead drunk, and she almost waited too long.'

'That's not enough to focus on him?'

'It's nothing! The woman was there! Without her testimony, for all we know the kid *could* have fallen down the stairs onto the hot plate!'

'Martin! What would the hot plate be doing at the bottom of the stairs? And how could she have landed on it in a perfect sitting position and stay there until she'd suffered third-degree burns and branded herself? And why would the hot plate be turned on in the middle of the night?'

'OK, Jennifer, the man is guilty, all right? I know it. You know it. Social Services knows it. Cornelia Lauren knows it. Heaven knows Heather knows it. And you can bet Elliott knows it too.'

'Then why can't anything be done? I don't understand it.'

'It's the system, Jenn.'

'The system! Martin, this sounds like a B movie! Everyone's powerless to fight the system?'

'I tried! I offered to take those kids into my own home! You've got to have a smoking pistol, or the next best thing, in court. I go in there with circumstances and shouting in the night, and I'll come out with an acquittal.

That's worse than no indictment in the first place. I'm trying to get the District Attorney to indict now, but we can't use Wyatt Oliver's history.'

'Why not?'

'Because according to the law, if he wasn't convicted, it never happened.'

'Let me change subjects here for a minute, Martin. How do you know Heather Lauren didn't return from preschool Monday?'

'You got our official statement. It came right off Mrs. Lauren's written statement.'

'May I see that?'

'The written statement?'

'Yes.'

'You promise not to quote directly from it?'

'Of course.'

Sergeant Grom dug it out from a pile in the middle of his desk, leafed through it, and produced a photocopy of a thick, handwritten sheaf. Jennifer scanned it quickly until she came to the following:

> I send Heather of to scool at 12:30. She
> dont com home at 2.30 lik everday. I
> wate and wate and send Elliott to lok.

'Did you check this out?' Jennifer asked.

'I assume someone corroborated it.'

'Who?'

'I don't know. We have a lot of people on this, Jenn.'

'Has anyone talked to her preschool classmates?'

'What do three- and four-year-olds know that can help us?'

'That she wasn't at school that day.'

Grom stared at her, unblinking. 'She never made it to school?'

'Did you talk to the preschool teacher?'

'I assume someone did.'

'You're assuming too much, Martin. I talked to her, and no one from the police department has asked her anything.'

'And she's saying the kid didn't make it to preschool that day?'

'She's saying Heather hadn't been coming for weeks. She didn't expect her that day.'

'What's this woman's name?'

'Angela Liachi.'

'I'll check it out. Liachi, you say?'

'Liachi.'

'We've got something on her.'

'Meaning what?'

'We got a complaint about her.'

'From whom?'

'Are you ready for this? From Wyatt Oliver.'

'You're serious?'

'Yeah. Just a minute. Hank!'

'Yeah!'

'Bring me that complaint Wyatt Oliver filed on the Liachi woman, will ya?'

Jennifer could hear grumbling from over the partitions as a podgy, grimy detective brought in a manila folder. 'In uniform today, huh Sarge?' he said.

Grom grunted and thanked him. He shuffled back out.

'Here it is,' Grom said, sitting again and picking his way through the carbon paper. 'Threatened my life,' he read, 'said she would kill me if she saw another bruise on one of my kids. I don't have to take that from anyone, blah, blah, blah.'

'So what'd you do with it?'

'Sent somebody over to tell her that a threat on someone's life was illegal and that she could be charged with assault, not to mention battery, manslaughter, and/or murder if she ever followed through with her threats.'

'She deny making them?'

'No. Told us if we wouldn't do our job relating to Wyatt Oliver, she would. We don't make a big deal of this type of a thing. We try to get the parties to talk and resolve their differences. In this case, it was apparent that that would not be the best approach, so we just let it drop.'

'Is that why you never asked her to corroborate the mother's story? You were afraid she would do something drastic?'

Martin studied her. 'You have a lot of insight,' he said.

'And you guys are pretty naïve. You think she wouldn't find out about the murder unless you told her?'

He was taken aback. 'Are you turning on me, Jenn?'

'I'm not turning on you, Martin. But I'm saying you've got more than enough to lock up Wyatt Oliver.'

'You gonna say that in the paper?'

'I don't know. Probably.'

'That's gonna make us look bad, Jennifer.'

'You *do* look bad, Martin.'

'I've got to ask you not to do it.'

'I can't make any promises.'

'It'll be the end of our friendship, Jennifer. It'll be the end of any information you get outta me.'

'Do you think I care about any of that, Sergeant? I want to be objective. I want to play this straight. I don't want to be a crusader, and it's not my place to tell you what to do or how to do it. But I have to tell you, you've got a woman and a child living with a murderer who should have been locked up months ago. I don't know how you can sleep at night, Martin. I should think you'd have Heather Lauren's blood on your hands.'

He stood quickly and glared down at her, and she knew she'd been too harsh. *Who do you think you are?* she asked herself. *One day with a column assignment and you start accusing cops of killing kids!* She raised both hands to him. 'I went too far, Martin. I'm sorry —'

But he wasn't listening. His intercom had buzzed, and he pushed the lever to answer. 'What is it?' he bellowed.

'A death, possible homicide, forty-three twenty-six West Stivers.'

Jennifer gasped and stood as Grom came charging around the desk, pulling his dress blue coat off the hook. She found herself in his way, but only temporarily. He clubbed her just below the neck with the back of his hand on his way out and knocked her back into her chair without even looking at her.

Her elbow had banged the arm of the chair and throbbed. She caught her breath and jumped up to follow Grom, but as she neared the front door, he was already climbing into an idling squad car. She sprinted the half block to her car and gave chase, but she lost him and had to rely on her memory to get to the Oliver-Lauren residence.

She screeched to a stop a block away and found the 4300 block cordoned off by squad cars, an ambulance, and several unmarked squad cars.

People were streaming from the surrounding buildings to as close to the scene as they could get. Jennifer joined them, wondering who Oliver had killed this time. As she neared the roped off area, she saw Elliott Lauren in the back seat of a squad car with a woman she assumed was Cornelia Lauren.

She made her way to the car and asked the woman to wind down the window. 'Are you Cornelia Lauren?' she asked the ashen face.

The woman nodded, but the officer at the wheel lurched around and shouted, 'Hey! Get away! Wind up that window!'

'I'm with the press,' Jennifer said.

'Get away!'

At least *they* were safe. She moved to the edge of the rope and stared to crawl under. 'You can't come in here, lady,' a cop told her.

'I'm Press,' she said.

'I don't care if you're the Queen of England,'

he said. 'Nobody but police are allowed in here right now.'

'What happened, Officer?'

'Somebody got snuffed, that's all I know.'

'Did Wyatt Oliver do it?'

'I didn't hear any names. Clear the way!'

Forensics were jogging up the path, with cameras and black boxes at their sides. Jennifer knew that as soon as they had marked the spot where the body had been found, they'd release it, and it would be carried out.

'You really don't know if the perp has been apprehended or who was murdered?'

The cop shook his head and ignored her.

In a few minutes, plainclothes detectives escorted a middle-aged black man from the apartment building. He was not handcuffed, so apparently he would simply be questioned. He stared at Jennifer as they approached, and as they passed, he shouted:

'That's her! That's her! That's the chick I saw in the house the last time I saw Oliver alive!'

9 A detective with the black man told the uniformed policeman, 'Don't let her out of your sight,' and kept moving.

'Hey, Officer, uh —'

'Officer Huber, ma'am, please stay right here with me.'

'Officer Huber, you don't have to worry about me. I'm Jennifer Grey with the *Chicago Day*. I was here earlier, yes, but on assignment. I saw Oliver, but —'

'So, who's Oliver? The dead man?'

'I assume, yes, but —'

'I know nothing about the case, lady. I just can't let you outta my sight.'

'Well, listen, when people come out of that house, I may be moving up and down the line here asking them questions. Can I do that?'

He looked worried.

'I'll keep waving at you to let you know I'm still here,' she said. 'Fair enough?'

'I don't know.'

'Here, take my wallet, better still, take my car keys. I can't get far without these.'

'Lady, I don't want any of your stuff. You just stay right here, 'cause I'm gonna hafta answer for you.'

Martin Grom emerged from the building, leading another couple of cops and the paramedics, who wheeled a trolley containing a covered body. The crowd edged forward. Jennifer felt strange, being the only media person on the scene. They'd be here soon enough, she decided.

'Who's the dead man, Sergeant?' she called.

'You know who he is, Jennifer,' Grom growled.

'See, Officer Huber, I know the sergeant.'

He just stared at her.

'Martin,' she called, grabbing his arm and slowing him, 'will you tell this guy I can be trusted?'

Grom was disgusted. 'What's the trouble?' he asked.

'The black guy they're questioning says he saw her here before the murder,' Huber explained. 'Cap'n Halliday told me to keep an eye on her.'

'I was here for a few minutes before going to see Angela Liachi, Martin,' Jennifer said. 'She can prove I wasn't here when Oliver was killed.'

'Don't kid yourself, Jenn,' Martin said. 'Angela Liachi is our prime suspect.'

Jennifer was speechless. *Of course*, she realized, *a person who had made a definite threat and was even named in a complaint would have to be the first suspect.* There had been a prerequisite to her threat — harm to one of the Lauren kids — and that had been fulfilled. Could Angela have been worked up to such a frenzy by their chat that she had actually followed through with her plans? Jennifer couldn't believe it.

'Then can I go?' she called after Grom.

'Just stay accessible, you hear?' he yelled back.

She nodded.

'It's all right, Huber!' Grom added. 'We know where to find her.'

Several other uniformed and plainclothes cops emerged from the building. 'How'd he die?' Jennifer asked.

'No comment.'

'Angela Liachi the only suspect?'

The men looked at each other and at her. 'We have no suspects as yet.'

'How'd he die?' she asked again, hoping someone in the back of the group had not heard the 'no comment' from the front.

'Fork,' someone said.

'Fork?'

'Fork to the back.'

'Common kitchen utensil?'

'You got it.'

'From his own house?'

'Can't tell yet.'

'Fingerprints?'

'Don't know yet.'

'Where was he found?'

'On the landing between the ground and first floors.'

'Happen there?'

'Probably outside his door on one.'

'Thank you. May I go in?'

'Not till the forensics come out.'

'His wife and child see the murder?'

'No comment.'

'She a suspect?'

'No suspects yet.'

Jennifer, as was her custom at such scenes, returned to her car and waited for the crowd to disperse. There wasn't much to see once the body had been removed, and people generally drifted away, just as the broadcast media rolled up to take long shots of the building.

After about twenty minutes, TV camera crews began setting up out front in the growing darkness, their lights illuminating street reporters in front of the building, reading sombre messages from cue cards, telling of the bizarre slaying of a man whose daughter had been found in this very building the day before, and whom many had considered a suspect in that death.

Jennifer walked around the block and came through the back alley to the side door. The cops supposed to be watching that door were ogling the TV reporters at the front. She took in the scene and casually walked through the open door and up the steps, careful to touch nothing.

Forensics were crouched everywhere, dusting for prints and tracks, taking blood samples from the stairs. They basically ignored her except to direct her around the areas where they worked.

She began to realize the idiocy of walking through the scene of a crime in which she herself was a suspect, but she was more overcome with the sense of evil in this place. She'd been at murder scenes before. But never this soon after the event.

She believed Satan was the author of death, the robber of life, and when a murder motivated by anger or hatred was perpetrated with such horrible violence, it carried the stench of evil. A feeling of fear and dread was almost physical in the place.

She prayed silently as she mounted the stairs. *Lord, protect me, cleanse me, be with me.*

The door to the Oliver-Lauren apartment was open, and the lights were off. 'Have you been in there yet?' she asked the forensics.

'No, ma'am. Not yet.'

She hurried back down the steps and out the door, drawing a surprised look from Officer Huber, who was now stationed at the side of the building. 'Good evening, Officer,' she said. He nodded.

Jennifer couldn't make it all compute. Why would the apartment door be open and the lights off? If Cornelia Lauren had been the perpetrator, wouldn't she have done it while he slept? Had she been there when it happened? If so, she would have either seen or had a good idea who had murdered Wyatt Oliver.

Had Elliott been home? Was he capable of such an act? She doubted it. Surely he could have had a motive if he had been treated as his sister had. But he was so small, and Oliver was so strong. Maybe, if he had surprised the man — But with a fork? Unlikely. The fork pointed to Cornelia. But what was it that Jennifer had seen in the back seat of the squad car? A bag of groceries? Had she been out and discovered him when she returned? Who would know?

Jennifer went back out into the alley and to the other side of the building next door. She rapped on the door and jumped back as a black face appeared immediately at the window. *Of course,* she realized, *everyone's been watching everything.*

'Excuse me,' she said, 'but could I ask you a few questions?'

'Depends on who you are,' said a male voice.

'I'm Jennifer Grey of the *Chicago Day*.'

'If I talk to you, I might be in the paper?'

'You might be, unless you don't want to be.'

'I do. Come on in.'

Jennifer hesitated, knowing immediately that her hesitation would probably offend the man. She walked in slowly and up a short flight of stairs to a tiny kitchen. The man, who looked to be in his early twenties, was long and lanky and wore a new white T-shirt and blue jeans with no belt. He was barefoot.

'Chair?' he said, pointing to a vinyl covered, aluminium framed one.

'Thank you.'

'Coffee?'

'Thank you.'

He scowled as if he'd wished she'd said no, and moved toward the stove.

'Oh, if it's any trouble —' she said.

'No trouble,' he said, unconvincingly.

'You don't mind talking to me and being quoted in the paper?'

'Are you kidding?' he said. 'Might be the highlight of my life.'

She smiled. 'Name?'

'Lionel Whalum,' and he spelled it for her.

'Age?'

'Twenty-five.'

'Occupation?'

'None.'

'You live here alone?'

'Nobody lives in this neighbourhood alone,' he said, sitting across from her and waiting for the kettle to boil.

'Family?'

'I live here with my mother and her brother. We're the only people on this block without kids.'

'Can you tell me what you saw today?'

'Everything.'

'Meaning?'

'I saw you earlier today.'

'You did? You did see everything then, didn't you?'

'Yes, ma'am.'

'What else did you see?'

'You mean around the time Oliver snuffed it?'

'Uh huh.'

'Kids were playing all over the place. Elliott was with them.'

'How far from his apartment?'

'Down the block.'

'Where was Mrs. Lauren?'

'His old lady? She was out with somebody from Social Services.'

'How do you know that?'

'I saw the car. Someone from the agency comes every now and then and takes her shopping, showing her how to get more food for less money, that kinda stuff. They do the same for us.'

'And then they brought her back when?'

'They didn't bring her back. She walked home.'

'Is that normal?'

'Yeah. Store's not that far away. They come for you because they know you probably wouldn't show up otherwise. But they don't have to take you home too.'

'Does this happen on some kind of a schedule?'

'Yeah, but nobody knows what it is 'cept Social Services. They just call and say they're coming to take you to the store, and it's usually within a few days after you get your cheque.'

'Uh huh. Did you see who it was from Social Services?'

'No, I just saw Cornelia get in the car.'

'Did Elliott go along?'

'No, he went back into the house for a while. Then he came back out to play.'

'What else did you see today, Lionel?'

'I saw another reporter. At least, I think he was a reporter.'

'What did he look like?'

'Big, tall. Young. Dark hair. Big glasses. Wore boots. Walked around the front of that building and took a lot of notes. I don't know if he actually went in or not, 'cause from where I am I can only see the front and the side paths and the back alley, I can't actually see the side door.'

'Was this guy wearing a denim suit?'

'Right. You know him?'

'I think so.' She certainly did. It sounded like Bobby Block. *What would he have been doing there? Maybe murdering Wyatt Oliver and trying to make it look like I did it? Good grief, Jennifer, you're paranoid. The kid is a scoundrel, but he wouldn't go that far to get your job!*

'What did you see me do today?'

'I knew you went inside because I saw you go around the side and heard you holler at Elliott. And then you didn't turn up in the back alley or come back out the front until you came running. I reckoned you must've met up with Oliver in there. I was hoping you'd killed him, but I saw him out the back about a half hour later.'

'You'll swear to that?'

'Sure.'

'And he was healthy?'

'Yeah!'

'And the other reporter came when?'

'While Mrs. Lauren was gone.'

'You see anybody else?'

'I saw the preschool teacher.'

'Angela Liachi?'

'Uh huh.' He made the coffee.

'When was this?'

'I saw her two or three times. Mid-afternoon, before Mrs. Lauren left. Then while she was gone.'

'Did she go into the building?'

'I don't think so. I saw her at the front and back, but never at the side.'

'What was she doing?'

'Just talking to the kids and watching them and roaming. Just like always.'

'How do you know her, Mr. Whalum?'

'We know everybody who comes through here. It's safer that way.'

'I suppose it is.'

'For everybody 'cept Wyatt Oliver anyway. We don't do much to protect that man.'

'Apparently not.'

'Can you blame us?'

'Do you think he killed Heather?'

'Everybody knows that. He's been beatin' those kids since they moved in here.'

'Who found him today?'

'She did.'

'She?'

'His old lady, Cornelia. She came back from the store with a bag of groceries, waved "hi" to Elliott, and the next thing I know she's out the front of the building screaming to call the police, call the police.'

'Did you call?'

'Me? No. I got enough trouble with the police. I don't need that. Anyway, there's enough people in her building to call. They never go anywhere.'

'There didn't seem to be anyone there when I was there.'

'They don't come to the door unless they know you. And they wouldn't have called the police for him.'

'I thought you said they would.'

'They would for her. Not for him. If it was him yelling to call the police, they'd have just shut the doors. They like her. She's a good person.'

'So then what happened?'

'Elliott came running to his mum, and she liked to tackle him to keep him outta that building. She set the grocery bag down and grabbed him in both arms and held on for all she was worth until the cops got here. That's when I knew Oliver musta snuffed it and was lyin' in there somewhere. 'Course, news travels fast, so soon enough I got the story.'

'What *is* the story?'

'People in my building think someone in his building got him with his own cutlery. This gonna be in the paper?'

10

'I've just been sitting here reading, wondering when I would hear from you,' Jim said when Jennifer called.

'I assume you've heard what's going on,' she said.

'Yeah. You need an ear?'

'I most certainly do, Love. But it might be kinda late. I've got two pieces to write tonight, and I have to talk my way out of being a suspect in this thing myself.'

'*That* I hadn't heard!'

'I saw Wyatt Oliver before he was murdered, and I was seen. But I'm not worried about that. I'll tell you all about it later. Can I call you and meet you somewhere?'

'Sure.'

'How late?'

'You name it. I'm off tomorrow, remember?'

'Oh, that's right! Thanks, Sweetheart. I'll call you as soon as I can.'

Jennifer had broken a boot heel in the alley behind the Oliver apartment building, so while she was in the phone booth, she decided to let Leo know she would be stopping at her apartment on the way in.

'You know the cops are looking for you?' he said.

'Yeah. Who called?'

'The redhead from the West Side. Is it serious?'

'Leo, for now I'm a suspect.'

'Tell me you're kidding.'

'I'm not. But I've also got a witness who saw me at the Oliver place and who also saw a healthy Wyatt Oliver after I left. And I was with Angela Liachi and then Nathalie Benedict and then Sergeant Grom the rest of the afternoon.'

'The cops are placing the time of death at late in the afternoon, Jennifer. Were you en route somewhere around that time?'

'Sure, I could have been going to or from any one of those appointments. I was with Grom when the report came in.'

'Did you go back to Oliver's late in the afternoon?'

'Not until after he was dead. That's where I'm calling from now.'

'Give me the details on your eyewitness, and I'll try to get you cleared through Grom. That'll give you time to run home on your way in if you want to, and I should at least be able to get you enough time to do your two pieces before they send you to Sing Sing.'

'Not funny, Leo.'

'Sorry. But don't dawdle.'

Jennifer knew the doorman at her building would keep an eye on her car, so she parked in front instead of in the underground garage and limped in the front door, gobbling a fast-food burger on the way.

'Your sister is waiting for you, ma'am,' the doorman said.

'My sister?'

'Yes, ma'am.'

'Thank you,' she said, looking warily into the lobby. From an overstuffed chair in the corner, peeking over the top of a magazine, were the fearful eyes of Angela Liachi. 'Angela!' Jennifer said, a little too loudly.

'Hi, Sis!' Angela said, making a show of embracing her. Then she whispered, 'I've got to talk to you!'

Jennifer took her upstairs while she changed into low-heeled shoes and freshened up. 'So, what are you doing here?' she asked, pointing Angela to the couch.

'I decided to take you up on your offer to get me out of that rat hole so I could cool off for a few days.'

'Angela!' Jennifer said, emerging from the bathroom. 'You know the police are looking for you?'

'I know. I did a very foolish thing, Jennifer.' Her voice grew husky and her eyes filled.

'Oh, please —' Jennifer said, dreading what she was about to hear.

'I shouldn't have even walked over there.'

'Angela, if you're about to make a confession, I —'

'It was a stupid thing to do,' Angela continued in a monotone, ignoring Jennifer and staring past her. 'I was in a foul mood after I talked to you. I thought about you sitting there with Nathalie Benedict and then going to see that homicide guy, and I knew you'd find out that they couldn't use the evidence they found by giving those phony physicals —'

'Angela, please, if, if, I don't even want to know right now if —'

'— and I knew that nothing would be done, because nothing ever gets done about people like Wyatt Oliver.' She began to cry.

Jennifer stood over her with her hands on Angela's shoulders. 'What are you going to do, Angela?'

'I want to stay here for a while. May I?'

'I have to get into the office to write my stories. Is one of them supposed to say that I'm harbouring the murderer of Wyatt Oliver?'

'I didn't say that, Jennifer! I *wanted* to kill him, but I couldn't bring myself to go inside! I hate myself because I didn't do it, but I'm glad it got done.'

Jennifer flinched. She had suppressed the same reaction to the murder, knowing all the while that it was a horrible thought. To be glad that a man has been plunged into eternity, and knowing that he certainly met a godless end —

'So you didn't do it.'

'No. Nathalie told me after my first episode with him, when I threatened him, that I would never really be able to do it.'

'You discussed it with her?'

'Sure. She said she thought she could do it if she felt as strongly about Oliver as I did, but she didn't think I could.'

'Dangerous talk.'

'I know. But, Jennifer, you haven't worked with the low-lifes in this city the way we have. You haven't faced the system. You haven't seen innocent people suffer and guilty people go free because of delays, adjournments, payoffs, deals, bargains, neglect, and incompetence.'

'Do you think Nathalie Benedict could have murdered Wyatt Oliver?'

Angela buried her face in her hands. 'I don't know,' she said. 'I really don't.'

Jennifer looked at her watch. 'I need a commitment from you, Angela.'

'Hm?'

'I need you to look me in the eye and tell me you didn't see Wyatt Oliver today.'

'I didn't.'

'I want to believe you.'

'You can.'

'Based on what you're telling me, I'm going to take the risk of harbouring you for a few hours.'

'Harbouring me?'

'You're wanted by the police, Angela, and I know it. That means I'm protecting you from them. But let me tell you this: If they ask, I'll have to tell them the truth.'

'Could you call me and let me know if they're coming?'

'No, I couldn't do that. I shouldn't even do this, but if I give you to them, they'll detain me as well, and I've got work to do first.'

'What do you want me to do?'

'Just stay here. Don't answer the door, and don't answer the phone unless it rings seventeen times. If it does, that's me.'

'Thanks, Jennifer.'

'Don't be too quick to thank me. We both may regret this soon enough. I've got to call Leo. That reminds me. Don't use the phone.'

'I won't.'

Jennifer dialled. 'Leo, I'm leaving right now.'

'I'm surprised to hear from you, Jennifer. Grom says they're staking out the underground garage in your building right now.'

'Luckily, I parked in front, but I'd better hurry or they'll tow me away. They may be waiting down there for me now, or on their way up.'

'I don't like it, Jenn, and neither does Cooper.'

'Cooper knows about this?'

'He's got contacts everywhere. What are you going to do?'

'I'll do whatever you say, Leo.'

'You sure you can clear yourself in this deal?'

'Of course.'

'Grom says the eyewitness you quote is a known pimp.'

'Terrific, Leo. If I'm going to try to get there without them seeing me, I've got to go right now. If you want me to just turn myself in, I will.'

'Come on in. Let's see if you can get the stories done before we have to give you up.'

Jennifer ran to the door, pointed back at Angela and said, 'Remember what I told you. Just stay put. I may not be back until morning.'

'What?' Angela said, but Jennifer was gone, sprinting past the lifts — she was sure the police were on their way up — and down the far stairway. She ran down nine flights of stairs, fearing at every turn that she would see cops who were supposed to be in the basement garage.

When she reached street level, she peered around the exit door a half block south to the front windows where the doorman was pointing two uniformed policemen to the lifts. Apparently they had not seen her car yet or were convinced that she was upstairs. She ran to her car and drove to the office.

Cooper and Stanton and Bobby Block were waiting for her when she got out of the lift at the far end of the city room. 'Follow me,' Leo said, and they headed for a small office that formerly housed the news wires and now was used for paper storage. A video display terminal had been plugged in.

'We're going to stall them for as long as we can,' Cooper said, 'but as soon as your stories are written, we're going to turn you over to them.'

'You're going to stand by me, aren't you?'

'Of course we are,' the big boss said. 'If you say you're innocent, you're innocent. But we can't hide someone who's wanted by the police, and we won't. At least, not for long.'

'I have a question for Bobby,' Jennifer said.

Bobby squinted at her. Leo and Cooper looked at him.

'Any reason you can't do the straight story?' she asked.

He shrugged.

'What's she talking about, Block?' Leo said.

'How should I know? Ask her.'

'Watch your mouth, Kid. You're talking to your boss's boss in front of his boss,' Max Cooper said, showing a remarkable familiarity with the hierarchy.

'Well, I don't know what she's talkin' about!' Bobby whined.

'Why were you at the scene of the murder today, Bobby?' she asked.

'Who says I was?'

'I do.'

'Are you saying you weren't?' Leo said.

'Well, no —'

'Then why were you? You weren't assigned!'

'Well, somebody has to handle the police beat while Susie Columnist here is posturing for the publisher!'

Everyone fell silent, but Max Cooper was hot. His forehead and ears reddened. Finally, he said, 'Leo, I don't want to see this person any more. Get rid of 'im.'

Leo and Bobby headed down the passage, leaving old man Cooper with Jennifer for a moment. 'Write me a good column, huh?' he said. 'Leave out anything about you bein' a suspect; we'll deal with that. The straight piece oughta write itself. Put your energy into the column, 'cause it's your column that's gonna make this paper over the next few years.'

He winked at her and left, and while she was flattered by his confidence, she hadn't decided to accept his long-term column offer, and she could have as easily burst into tears and begged for twelve solid hours' sleep as try to write.

Besides not knowing what to think about the fact that her salvation from being a suspect was in the hands of a known pimp, she wanted to see Jim and talk to him about all the dangling clues in the case.

Neither did she know yet whether Angela Liachi had been straight with her. For all Jennifer knew, Angela *had* murdered Wyatt Oliver. Jennifer's conscience was already nagging her for protecting Angela from the police, guilty or not. The same was true of her own flight from Sergeant Grom.

For a minute she toyed with insisting that Cooper and Leo turn her in, but at the same time she was nudging the elements of her column around in her head. As they fell into place, she began writing:

I'm facing difficult emotions as I

compose these words. The man most people assume murdered four-year-old Heather Lauren has himself been murdered, not a full day after I championed capital punishment for whoever had done it.

And so now what am I supposed to think? How am I supposed to react? How are you reacting? Cornelia Lauren may now feel free to tell what really happened in that home, fearing no reprisal from her common-law husband.

It won't surprise anyone to learn that Wyatt Oliver tortured the girl, let her go too long without eating, intimidated her mother to the point that she couldn't even protect her own daughter, went too far with his methods, and wound up killing Heather.

We'll find that he carried her to the basement of the apartment building in the middle of the night, probably Monday, and tied the lifeless body to a post — for there are no signs of struggle or blood in that basement now — and attempted to make it look as if she had been abducted.

We'll find that she died from shock, but that any of several injuries inflicted on that vulnerable, defenceless little frame could have done her in. And then we'll be glad that the perpetrator got his.

Or will we? When we know for sure it was Wyatt Oliver, will we still be glad he's dead? You see my dilemma? If he murdered Heather Lauren, I'm glad justice was done. But the justice was not carried out in a just way.

There was no trial. So, unless Cornelia Lauren, one of two people in the world with firsthand knowledge of the first slaying, committed this murder, the perpetrator was making assumptions. And evidence will surface to clear Mrs. Lauren.

I spent time today with several people who are so frustrated with the "system" in this city, the bureaucracy that favours the guilty and harms the innocent, that any of them could have had a motive to murder Wyatt Oliver. By the time I finished talking with them, I shared their feelings.

I saw Wyatt Oliver alive today. I left him with no shadow of a doubt that he had killed his own daughter. It's a strange feeling to see a man a few hours before he meets a violent death. And I wrestle with the emotion that tells me that as one who believes in the sovereignty of God, one who believes that vengeance is His, one who believes that God is the author of life and that Satan is the author of death, I should not have any positive feeling whatsoever related to the death of a child abuser.

I'll keep praying about it; and I don't say that flippantly.

11

Jennifer was in the middle of tapping out the straight update article on the entire case when Leo knocked at the door.

'They're here,' he said. 'We've admitted you're here, and we've promised that you'll go with them if we can just let you finish your story. If you need it for the piece, Mrs. Lauren has been cleared, and she has named Oliver as Heather's murderer.'

Jennifer was surprised half an hour later when she entered the city room and was arrested by Martin Grom himself. As he was quietly reading her her rights, Max Cooper caught her eye from behind the sergeant and pointed to Gerald Mayfield, the newspaper's counsel.

Jennifer was flabbergasted that they would

have thought to call him and ask him to represent her. 'I have counsel,' she said. 'Thank you.'

Grom was surprised too. Mayfield introduced himself. 'This isn't so magnanimous as it seems, Mrs. Grey,' Mayfield said. 'I happened to be in the Loop tonight anyway.'

'Still, I'm grateful.'

'Don't mention it. Sergeant, may my client and I have a few minutes?'

'Well, I gotta tell you, Counsellor, my partner is waiting in the car, and the people here have been harbouring this woman for quite some time —'

'Martin, you told me earlier that it was OK and that you knew where to find me,' Jennifer said.

'Yeah, but when we looked at your place, all we found was Angela Liachi. We'll have to bust you for harbouring her, at least.'

'Well,' Mayfield said, 'which is it? Are you arresting her on suspicion of murder or for harbouring a suspect?'

'We haven't decided yet.'

'Then while you're thinking about it, surely you wouldn't mind if my client and I spent a few minutes in private.'

Grom shrugged, grimacing.

Jennifer and the dapper Mayfield wended their way through clusters of desks and tables to the far end of the huge city room, finally sitting across from each other on a desk top. 'I'm so sorry about this,' Jennifer said. 'It's all my fault, and I know I shouldn't have gone to the Oliver place today, and —'

'Just hold on a minute, Mrs. Grey. The worst thing you've done so far is to let this Liachi woman stay in your place. If she's guilty, that'll compound matters.'

'She isn't.'

'You can't know that.'

'I'm pretty sure.'

'Well, I should hope so.'

'There's something strange going on here, Mr. Mayfield. Sergeant Grom said his partner was waiting in the car. Does it make sense that the numbers one and two men from West Side Homicide would be here looking for me? It seems anyone could come and round me up.'

'True enough. So what are you saying?'

'I'm worried about Martin.'

'Martin?'

'Grom, the sergeant. He's been very distraught since we spoke today. This case is really getting to him.'

'That uniformed sergeant is the Homicide Chief on the West Side?'

'Yes.'

'And his assistant would be whom?'

'Hank Henry.'

'And Grom works for whom?'

'Captain Halliday, I believe, Chief of Investigative Operations.'

'You have the number for the West Side Precinct?'

Jennifer recited it to him.

'Good evening. Gerald Mayfield of Bransfield, Mayfield, and Beckman calling for Captain Halliday, please…John? Gerry

112

Mayfield here. How you doing?...Good! Me too. Listen, do you have a minute?...Yeah, I know. I'm involved in it too now. I'm representing the *Day* and their reporter Jennifer Grey...Yes, she's been arrested actually. John, can you tell me who's heading up this investigation for you?...Oh, *you* are. Well, what about your Homicide Chief over there, Sergeant, uh...right, Grom. What's he doing?...Excuse me just a minute, John.

'Jennifer, Halliday tells me he's given Grom the rest of the night off. Says he's taken control of the operation himself.'

She raised her eyebrows.

'John, the man is here right now. He's handling the arrest of Mrs. Grey himself. Is that what you want, or can I bring her over to you myself?...Sure, hang on.'

Mayfield hurried over to Martin Grom and told him he was wanted on the phone. After a few minutes of intense conversation with his boss, Grom stormed out of the city room. Mayfield took the phone again.

'What's his problem, John?...Ah, I see. Five-year-old, huh? Good man though, right?...Sure. We'll be over. Thanks, John.'

Jennifer was puzzled.

'Let's go,' Mayfield said. 'We can talk in the car. I want you to tell me all about your day.'

'Happy to,' Jennifer said, following him out, 'but what's happening with Grom?'

'Well, seems he's a father himself. Bunch of boys and a five-year-old daughter.'

'I know.'

'That's why he's taking this case so personally. He's been working on it around the clock. It's been affecting him.'

'In what way?'

'Halliday says Grom wore his uniform today because he thought it was the day of the monthly meeting of the Fraternal Order of Police. But that's tomorrow.'

'An easy mistake.'

'Not for Grom. He's secretary of the Chicago chapter.'

'What pushed Halliday into sending Grom home?' Jennifer asked as they approached Mayfield's car.

Mayfield stood at the open door as she got in. 'When Grom and Henry brought the Liachi woman in, she told Halliday she'd never been questioned about Heather Lauren, even though Mrs. Lauren said she never came home from preschool.'

'And?'

'Halliday was upset. To him, that was a major omission by a homicide sergeant, and he thought it was time Grom got some rest. They're all getting a lot of heat from downtown, and somebody is holding Halliday himself responsible for getting the thing cleared up.'

'Am I going to be spending the night locked up, Mr. Mayfield? If I am, I need to call my boyfriend.'

'I think you'll be able to see your boyfriend tonight, Jennifer. I'll try to have you out of there on your own recognizance — or mine — as soon as possible. John Halliday and I are old buddies.'

Jennifer tried to give Gerald Mayfield every detail of her day, recreating much of it from her notes. He was not happy about her having entered the crime scene before the forensics had finished.

'You know they have fantastic equipment,' he said. 'They'll find some trace of you there.'

'Well, as I said, I had been there earlier in the day, too. And the forensic men *saw* me there, so there won't be any hiding that.'

'I don't want to hide it. But if you hadn't been there at all, and there was therefore no trace that you had been there, they'd be hard pressed to try to say you had anything to do with Oliver's murder. You were there before *and* after, so who's to say you weren't there during?'

'You are.'

Mayfield laughed. 'True enough. But you've made my job a bit more difficult than it needed to have been.'

'I'm sorry.'

'Nonsense. I enjoy the challenge. You are innocent, aren't you?'

'Pardon me?'

'You are innocent, are you not? You didn't murder Wyatt Oliver, did you?'

'What do you think?'

'I think I'd better coach you on how to answer a direct question. I am not kidding when I ask you that, and neither will John Halliday be kidding. And you can be sure he will ask you. People will be asking you that, and every time you are asked, you would serve yourself well by looking the interrogator in the eye and telling him the truth.'

'Even if I'm guilty?'

'Even more so. You'll notice that I didn't tell you what to say; I just said to tell the truth.'

'I didn't murder Wyatt Oliver, Mr. Mayfield.'

'Thank you. That was encouraging. Do you know who did?'

'No, sir.'

'Very good. Do you have an idea who did?'

'I have fears.'

'Care to speculate?'

'I don't know. There are so many people who wanted to. Myself included.'

'It would be good if no one else in an official capacity heard you say that.'

'But it's the truth.'

'Fine, but if you are innocent and want others to believe you, you'll keep quiet about your own motive, means, and opportunity. You see, the fact that you were at the scene before and after means that you had the opportunity. Everybody in town had a motive, it seems. The means? Well, someone who was in that apartment got to the table or cutlery drawer in time to use a fork on Oliver, probably to make it look as if his wife did it.'

'I worry about Nathalie Benedict and Angela.'

'So do I. Using a fork could be construed as a feminine means of attack.'

'But I'm talking about the timing,' Jennifer

said. 'It had to be someone who had access to the schedule of when Social Services was taking Mrs. Lauren shopping.'

'A good point,' Mayfield said. 'I'm surprised too that Oliver would let his wife out of the house, since she was the one person who knew that he had murdered Heather.'

'He probably had her convinced that she was as much at fault and that if he got in trouble for it, she would too.'

'Yeah, but mother-love usually transcends things like that,' he said, 'especially after the daughter is gone.'

'Who knows?' Jennifer said. 'Maybe she *was* getting ready to spill the beans.'

'Have you ruled out the son?'

'Elliott? Too small.'

'Means, motive, opportunity,' Mayfield reminded her.

'I don't think so.'

'Neither do I, but don't overlook anyone. Including your eyewitness.'

'*My* eyewitness? The pimp? How much help is he going to be?'

'His record and his occupation have little to do with his credibility.'

'They should, Mr. Mayfield. That's another problem with the system.'

'For now, don't knock it. He may be the only one who can clear you.'

12 As Gerald Mayfield and Jennifer entered the West Side Precinct station house, Jennifer caught sight of Jim waiting in the lobby. She ran to him.

'I heard about it on the radio,' he said.

'Heard about what?'

'Bobby got fired.'

'Yes, and — ?'

'And he's gone to the news media saying that you're the prime suspect, that you went crazy with all the publicity today's column brought you, and you acted out your fantasy of capital punishment on the murderer of the child.'

Jennifer was speechless. Jim held her.

'I suppose this bearer of good news is Jim,' Mayfield muttered.

'Yes, I'm sorry,' Jennifer said, making the introductions.

'Nice to meet you, Mr. Purcell. So what else did Bobby say?'

'He said another suspect was found in Jennifer's apartment and that there is speculation about conspiracy. Sounds crazy.'

'It *is* crazy,' Mayfield said. 'We'd better go in, Jennifer. You'll probably have to wait, Purcell.'

Before ushering Mayfield and Jennifer into Captain Halliday's office at the back of the building, the desk sergeant told Mayfield he had a message to call Leo Stanton at the *Day*. The conversation was brief, but after Mayfield hung up, he said, 'We'll be initiating litigation against your former assistant, of course.'

'Of course,' Jennifer said.

Captain Halliday in many ways reminded Jennifer of an older Sergeant Grom. He didn't have the same mannerisms, and was in fact almost grandfatherly, but he was a large, rangy man. His white hair was thinning, and his full face was rosy, eyes sparkly.

He didn't rise when they entered but rather sat back and sized them up over the tops of his half glasses while pointing to chairs. Mayfield walked round to shake Halliday's hand first.

'Good to see you again, Gerry. And Jennifer, we've met. And I've worked with your intended a time or two.'

'Oh really? Well, he's not really my intended, but —'

'Whatever, let's talk about why my crack homicide boys think you might have murdered this child killer, not that I wouldn't have wanted to do it myself.'

'You know, John, that's what everybody's been saying all day,' Mayfield jumped in. 'People who read Mrs. Grey's column this morning, and even people who didn't. It seems she can't run into anyone who doesn't share that sentiment.'

'Is that so? Well, I guess nobody loves somebody who could do something like that, do they? But nonetheless, we can't go around taking the law into our own hands, now can we?'

'Of course not,' Mayfield said, 'but —'

'Gerry, I'm gonna have to ask you to let Mrs. Grey here speak for herself.'

'Well, John, I appreciate that, but I am her counsel, and I prefer to represent her.'

'I don't mind, Mr. Mayfield,' Jennifer said.

'Yeah,' Halliday said, 'and any way, this isn't anything official. I just want to have an off-the-record chat. I won't hold anything you say against you in a court o'law, as we have to say these days, an' you don't quote me in the paper, fair enough?'

'Sure!'

'Uh, can we stipulate something here, John?' Mayfield said. 'I need to feel very comfortable here, as you're trying to make us feel, I think —'

Halliday winked at Jennifer, 'These lawyers are never comfortable unless they're stipulatin' something, are they? All right, Gerry, just what is it you want stipulated?'

'I want to clarify that this is not an official interrogation and that nothing my client says here can or will be used against her in court.'

Halliday swore and then excused himself to

Jennifer. 'Isn't that what I just said, Gerry? We go back a long way. You know me. I said I wanted to clear this up. I don't want any trouble with the media, and I don't want to detain this young lady any more than we have to. I said I wouldn't use anything against her, but I'll listen to everything that might clear her without further trouble. It's late, Gerry, and I'm sure we all want to go home. Don't you?'

'Yes, but —'

'Well, then just take me at my word like you've always known you could. All right, I know it's out of the ordinary for a cap'n to talk to a suspect off-the-record after she's been read her rights; do I hafta admit that Grom was way out of line to be bustin' somebody after I tol' him to go home? OK, let's get on with this, and I'm stipulatin' whatever it is you said, which I had already said. Let's work on getting this over with so I don't have to deal with a false arrest charge and you don't have to worry about court.'

'I'll stipulate *this*,' Mayfield said. 'If we leave here tonight with no charges pending, there'll be no false arrest claim. And I haven't even cleared that with my client.'

'OK with me,' Jennifer said.

'Good,' Halliday said. 'Can we finally begin?'

They both nodded, smiling.

'I must tell you,' the old man began, 'that even though my little homicide crew is distraught and overworked and has made its share of errors here lately, they don't lightly arrest someone on suspicion of murder. As I understand it, you have been placed at the scene of the crime.'

Jennifer nodded and started to speak. But Halliday continued.

'I'm also aware that one of the neighbours says he saw Oliver after you were there, and that he was healthy.'

'Yes, when I came running out of there the first time, it could have looked like I had done something wrong.'

'Well, it did. Do you have any idea how many people saw a well-dressed woman run from that building and speed away in her car? The next thing they know, it's several hours later and Oliver is dead. If this, uh, Whalum, Lionel Whalum, hadn't seen Oliver about mid-afternoon, you'd be in big trouble.'

'I'm glad you talked to him, because I was relieved when he told me —'

'Yes, I'm aware that you also talked to him. That was not a wise thing to do.'

'Why?'

'If you were aware of the man's profession, you wouldn't have wanted to be alone with him.'

'I'm aware now.'

'You saw his Cadillac with the multi-coloured headlamps and the fur-lined rear window?'

'No. Was it there?'

'It usually is.'

Hank Henry brought in some documents for

the captain. 'Did you get him home all right?' Halliday asked.

'Yes, sir,' Henry whispered. 'I'm sorry, sir, but I hadn't been apprised of the fact that he had been ordered off duty until he told me at the *Day* offices.'

'That's all right. I know how intent he is on solving this one.' He glanced at his watch. 'You got here fast. He still lives on the Near North Side, doesn't he?'

'Yes, sir, but he just had me drop him off at the Chevy dealer up here on Lester. He'd dropped his van off there this morning.'

'Surely they're not open this late, are they Hank?'

'No, sir. But he had extra keys, and they always let him settle up later.'

'It's after midnight, Hank. You goin' home?'

'Yes, sir, but I'd kinda like to see this thing wrapped up too, and I thought maybe if you had time, I could try out a few of my thoughts on you.'

'If you want to hang around, Hank, I'll be here. But if you head home, I'll understand.'

'I'll be here.'

'Dedicated man,' Halliday said. 'You deal with him much, Jennifer?'

She shook her head. Halliday leafed through the papers Hank Henry had delivered. He read, half aloud and half to himself, so Mayfield and Jennifer caught only bits and pieces:

> Blood on stairs not an hour old when
> forensics arrived. Door casing to Oliver

apartment had been shattered,
apparently by a kick just under the
doorknob. Lab tests show partial rubber
print of sole and heel indicate possible
oversized men's shoe, approximately
thirteen, extra wide, possible quad E.
Brand Apache Workmate.

'Good shoe. My dad wore 'em in the factory.
Used to use 'em on the street when he walked
the beats in the fifties. Not really regulation,
but they were comfortable. Never wore out.'

Door had knocked out jamb and swung
all the way to wall, where knob drove
hole into wall. Signs of struggle in the
kitchen, cutlery drawer open, blood on
kitchen table, living room rug, wall near
door, first floor landing, copious
amounts on stairs and banister, body
found on landing between ground and
first floor.

Coroner is estimating that the pound
strength required to drive common
kitchen fork through the latissimus dorsi
muscle and to break a rib and puncture
the heart would indicate that the
perpetrator was either unusually strong
or extremely agitated.

Halliday looked up. 'Well, that kinda goes
without saying, doesn't it? Somebody kicks
Oliver's door in, beats him to the cutlery
drawer, starts poking him in the back in the
kitchen, and chases him down a flight of stairs.

I'd say whoever it was was agitated, wouldn't you?'

He didn't wait for an answer.

> Coroner has determined eleven distinct
> puncture wounds, two to the deltoid
> muscle, seven to the latissimus, and two
> to the fleshy area in the lower right back.
> Assuming the victim was running away,
> the perpetrator was either significantly
> taller or inflicted all the wounds from a
> higher step on the stairs — unlikely
> because of the blood trail. Three of the
> puncture wounds affected the heart, and
> it's likely that the fatal blow was not the
> final wound, whatever that means.

'I suppose it means the murderer could have left after fewer stabs,' Mayfield said. Jennifer felt sick.

'You don't look tall enough or strong enough or agitated enough to have done this, Mrs. Grey,' Captain Halliday said. 'Did you murder the man?'

She looked him straight in the eye. 'No, sir, I did not.'

'May we go,' Mayfield asked.

'Not just yet. Let me see what else we've got here. Ah, interviews with neighbours in the building.

> No love lost. Heard the door breaking,
> assumed it was Oliver himself. He's
> done it enough times. Heard the
> scuffling, thought he might be punishing

the boy again. Heard feet running on the
stairs and the tumbling to the landing.
Heard male screaming, probably Oliver.
Heard heavy footsteps running out. Saw
no one.

'Yeah, I'll bet,' Halliday said, then he
continued.

Called cops? No. They never come for
disturbances with Oliver any more.
Frankly, wishing he would get it one of
these days. Thought maybe the wife did
it, but when she screamed for cops, it
was several minutes later.

Halliday peeked over his glasses again and
looked at Jennifer, then at Mayfield. 'The man's
lucky his wife showed up. The neighbours
probably would've just walked over him for a
few weeks. This frankly makes me wonder if
someone in the building didn't do it. Maybe a
bunch of them did it, just like the *Murder on
the Orient Express*.'
Halliday turned back to the report.

What did neighbours notice unusual that
day? Woman nosing around at about
noon, running away within the half
hour.

'That's you, huh?'

Preschool teacher wandering through as

usual, at least twice during the mid-
afternoon.

'We've got her locked up in the back. Lot
more points to her than you, frankly, but she
doesn't look any too tall or strong either.'

Tall young man in western wear looking
around, early afternoon.

'That one's worth checking out.'
Jennifer caught Mayfield's eye, but said
nothing.

Mrs. Lauren went shopping in Social
Services vehicle. Not unusual, except
driver appeared to be the director
herself, Mrs. Benedict.

'Don't know what to make of that. No one
says she was in the building at all.'

Neighbours in the building and next
door noticed police traffic at Whalum
residence, approximately 4:00 p.m.

'Wonder what this is?'

Kids in neighbourhood corroborate this,
and one also says he saw grey panel
truck type vehicle pull into back alley.
But no one else saw this, nor did youth
see it pull away. Also unemployed men
talking at corner saw unmarked squad

car at Whalum residence for
approximately twenty minutes.

Halliday looked agitated. 'Hank! You still
here?'

There was no response. Halliday grabbed his
phone and dialled the desk. 'Yeah, is Hank
Henry out there? Tell 'im I wanna see 'im!'

Henry came chugging back and was surprised to see that Jennifer and Mayfield were
still there.

'Sir?'

'These your notes?'

'Yes, sir.'

'Well, what'sis all about, police activity at
Whalum's around four o'clock? You tellin' me
there were cops there that close to the time of
the murder and we didn't hear or see anything?'

'At the time I wrote that, sir, I was unaware
of the time similarity. Apparently I could have
been in the neighbourhood not long before the
attack.'

'You?'

'Yes sir, it was me.'

'What were you doing at Whalum's, Hank?'

'Just putting a little heat on him, sir. Sergeant Grom, who used to deal with him a lot
when he was in the Vice Control Division, got a
call from VCD recently complaining that
Whalum was apparently plying his trade
unchecked on North Avenue and West Division. They were running the girls off, but they
couldn't get to Whalum.'

'So what was your assignment, Hank?'

'Grom asked if I would just pay him a call, mostly for looks. Let people see the unmarked squad in front of his place, embarrass him a little, that type of thing. I just talked to him for a while, told him the heat was on and that no one up here accepted any bribes or anything like that.'

'Sounds pretty small time when we're on a much more important case, Hank.'

'Yes, sir.'

'But that's not your problem. I'll take it up with Grom.'

'Frankly, sir, I didn't mind doing it. Sergeant Grom has had a lot on his mind, and with his daughter and all, he doesn't cater too much to, um, pimps, sir. He didn't want to handle it himself, and yet he didn't want to let down his friends in VCD.'

'I understand.' Halliday smiled. 'Sometimes it is kinda fun just to intimidate one of these bad guys, you know what I mean? Well, uh, Hank, what else did you get from the neighbours inside Oliver's building?'

'Not much. The one black guy, the one who saw Mrs. Grey here, he was very helpful. He's the one who called when Mrs. Lauren started screaming.'

'When does he say he saw Mrs. Grey?'

'Between twelve and one, just like everyone else.'

'Any other witnesses say they saw Oliver alive after that?'

'Yes, sir. At least three, including Whalum.

129

And some kids. The kids all know him. Scared of him. Hate him.'

'Ha!' Halliday said. 'Wonder if the kids did it?'

The captain stood and stretched, and Jennifer realized how tall the man was. He looked suddenly older and more tired than when they first came in. 'You've got enough witnesses that say they saw Oliver alive after you went runnin' away, young lady. That's good enough for me. Now I gotta ask you not to use anything you heard in here tonight in the paper. OK?'

'That won't be easy,' she said. 'It was most interesting.'

'But we have a deal, don't we? Your lawyer even stipulated it, remember?'

13 Jennifer had dark circles under her eyes and was dragging her feet on her way out to the lobby, but she was alert enough to ask Gerald Mayfield for one more favour.

'Sure, what is it?'

'Could you get them to release Angela? From what he just read, she doesn't have any more strength or whatever than I do.'

'I'll try, but it'll be tougher with her. She could have been agitated enough, and she is on record as having threatened the man.'

'Can we at least bail her out?'

'I'll check.'

It took another forty-five minutes, and Mayfield had to post a personal bond — 'based solely on your word, Jennifer; I don't know this woman' — but Angela was released. Jim offered to take her home and Jennifer back to her car at the *Day* office. Mayfield was grateful. 'I can't thank you enough, Mr. Mayfield,' Jennifer said.

'It was fun,' he said, heading for his car.

'Did I get you in a lot of trouble, Jennifer?' Angela asked in the car.

'Some. Not much. Most of it was my own doing. They're going to waive the harbouring charge. How are you doing?'

'Well, that wasn't my favourite way to spend a late evening. I was almost asleep. I wouldn't have bet a penny I'd be bailed out tonight. Good experience, though. Just taught me more about the crazy system.'

'We keep coming back to that, don't we?' Jennifer said.

'Yeah,' Angela said, but she was preoccupied, staring out the window.

Jennifer let her be for a few minutes, then asked what she was thinking.

'I'm a little scared, that's all.'

'You wanna stay with me tonight?'

'No, thanks, not that kind of scared. Scared of me.'

Jennifer wanted to pump her, but she was too tired, and she decided Angela was too, so she probably wouldn't elicit much. She was wrong.

'My reaction to this whole thing bothers me a lot,' Angela began suddenly. 'I've gone through moments when I wondered if I actually *had* murdered Wyatt Oliver. I rehearsed it so many times. Not with a fork, of course, but whatever was handy.'

She fell silent again, and Jennifer wondered

aloud if there was anyone within blocks of where Wyatt Oliver lived who didn't have a motive to kill him.

'Probably not,' Angela decided.

'And the one with the best motive of all didn't do it,' Jim offered.

'Cornelia Lauren?' Angela said. 'Don't be too sure. She's pretty shrewd in her limited way. She could have been planning this for a long time.'

'But this soon after her daughter's murder?'

'What better time?'

Jim waited on the street until Angela was safely inside her building. 'I'd love to hear every last detail,' he said as he pulled away, 'and I'm sure you're dying to tell me, Jenn, but you'd better save it.'

Jennifer lay her head on his shoulder, turned sideways in the seat, and slipped both her hands under his arm. 'Jus' wake me when we get to the office,' she slurred. 'I gotta talk to Leo for a minute.'

'He'll still be there?'

She nodded. 'He's putting the first section to bed.'

In the *Day* car-park a half hour later, Jim gently pulled his arm from her grasp and wrapped it around her shoulders. 'Sweetheart,' he said quietly.

'Um hum,' she said, eyes still closed.

'We're here.'

She opened her eyes without moving. 'So we

are,' she said. 'I'm comfortable. How 'bout you?'

He chuckled. 'Why don't you just let me drop you at your place, Jenn? You can talk to Leo tomorrow.'

'No,' she said, sitting up. 'It can't wait. What time is it?'

'Almost two o'clock.'

'Ouch. What time does the sun come up tomorrow morning?'

'You mean *this* morning? I don't know — about seven.'

'I'll check.'

And with that she dashed into the building and up to see Leo. 'Hey, hey!' Leo said. 'How's my little fugitive?'

'Bushed. I gotta talk to you.'

'Coffee?'

'Why not? It's too late to keep me up.'

He sent someone for two cups. 'So, talk to me.'

'You remember the agreement I made with you and Mr. Cooper about Jim and me and police reporting?'

'Yeah, you haven't violated that, have you?'

'No.'

'Good.'

'But I *would* like to know what you would do about the police beat if I left.'

'If you left!'

'I mean, if I left the police beat, not the paper. With Bobby gone —'

'He's gone all right. I shoulda dumped him

134

when he tried to get you in trouble the first
time.'

'Tried?'

'So, anyway, what would I do with the
police beat if you left? Frankly, I'd have my
pick of the news staff.'

'You would?'

'Yeah. I told Cooper I thought you'd take the
column —'

'You did?'

'Uh huh, and he suggested Bobby, but that
was before this evening. After that, he said he
would clear anyone I wanted, if they wanted to
come.'

'Got anybody in mind?'

'A few, yeah.'

'Yeah? Are you to the point where you'll be
disappointed if I stay?'

'I'll still be in charge of you, Jennifer, so I
don't care what you do.'

'You do!'

'You're right. I want you to take this column.
Your piece tonight was —'

'How badly do you want me to take it?'

'As badly as Cooper does.'

'Is that badly enough that you two slave
drivers will rescind our little agreement about
Jim and me?'

'You set me up!'

She laughed.

'I don't know,' he said.

'Come on, it's not the police beat. There'd be
no conflict of interest.'

'But your stories would often overlap with police stories.'

'Like now.'

'Right. What would you do then?'

'I'd use him.'

'You'd use Jim?'

'You bet I would.'

'And if we back off about you and Jim, you'll take the column?'

'I don't know yet. I haven't prayed about it or talked to Jim about it yet.'

'Will you?'

'I won't even consider it unless that agreement is eliminated.'

'If I told you it was eliminated right now, when would I get your answer about the column?'

'Soon. Do you have the power to rescind it?'

'Are you kidding? You ever see Cooper cross the Lion?' They both laughed. 'Forget the agreement,' he added.

'You mean it?'

He nodded.

'Thanks, Leo!'

'The competition will be good.'

'What do you mean?'

'C'mere, Jennifer. Let me give you a sneak preview of Jake Rogers's column, which will always appear opposite yours.'

Jennifer read Jake's column off the film that would make up the front page of the morning's paper. He played critic, evaluating her work as a police beat writer ('gushy, gee-whiz reporting'), her two personal columns ('amateurish, sensational, emotional, religious'), and even the placement of the column ('call it professional jealousy if you will, but it took me six years of paying my dues before my column was placed on the front page').

'I'm shocked.'

'Don't be. It's vintage Jake. And it's probably more entertainment than substance. I can't imagine he really feels that way, but he knows it'll sell papers.'

'I have to tell you, I would never even acknowledge in print that kind of criticism.'

'Of course you wouldn't, Jenn. If he keeps this up, we'll find out what the grassroots reader really wants.'

'I don't want to take the column to prove something to Jake. I hardly know the man, and I usually enjoy his stuff, especially the humour. This doesn't amuse me. But it does convince me that we're long overdue for an old-fashioned, conservative viewpoint.'

'You know we are, Jennifer. Let me know soon, will you?'

'Leo, there's a method to my madness here, and I don't want to get thrown off the track by Jake Rogers' venom. Even if I don't take the column, I want you to rescind the agreement I made about Jim and me immediately, for the sake of tomorrow's column.'

'You been working with him on something?'

'Of course not. I've lived up to my end of the bargain. But I'm about to ask him to help me with something. It may be crazy, but if it works, it could be a dynamite column. How 'bout it?'

'All right. But for tomorrow you're still writing two pieces, right? The straight one and the column.'

'Right.'

'And my pledge to you is that if you'll give me just forty-eight hours notice when you're going to take the column assignment, you'll be off the police beat immediately.'

'Thanks, Leo.'

Jim was dozing in the car and jumped when Jennifer opened the passenger side door. 'I'm sorry, Jim.' He smiled and drove toward her apartment building. 'You have plans for tomorrow?' she asked.

'Just sleeping in.'

'Can I spoil 'em?'

'You're the one thing I'd even give up sleeping in for. How's that for a sentence, Mrs. Hemingway?'

'It got the point across. I have a plan for tomorrow morning, before sunrise.'

He groaned.

'C'mon,' she said. 'You'll still get four hours or so of sleep. And it'll be fun. You still have your forensic kit from cadet training school?'

''Course. Cost me more'n a hundred bucks.'

'Got all the stuff?'

'Think so.'

'You're gonna need it.'

'You gonna get me in trouble?'

'No, unless there's something wrong with

going over a crime scene after the forensics have already been there.'

He thought a minute, parking in front of her building. 'I guess not. What else can you tell me?'

'Dress warmly. And be praying with me about my leaving the police beat and becoming a full-time columnist.'

'I will. I'll miss you.'

'Are you kidding? You'll see more of me than ever.'

'Apparently so. Are we going to be too tired for dinner tomorrow night?'

'Highly unlikely,' she said. And she kissed him good night.

14 It was cold in her apartment when Jennifer arose not four hours later. She liked to sleep with the window open slightly, even in the dead of winter. It made for good sleeping, but she paid dearly for it every morning on cold floors.

As she padded around the apartment in her bulky dressing-gown and slippers, she fought to keep her eyes open. Her breathing was deep and even, as if she were still in bed. But as she splashed cold water on her face and plugged in the coffeepot, her mind was racing.

She was convinced she would never get her eyes fully open and would probably look bed-raggled to Jim, but she was still high with excitement. She'd had things rattling around in her brain ever since the conversation the night before with Captain John Halliday. She quickly ran down in her mind the list of things she had to accomplish to get out the front door by six; then she put herself on automatic pilot so they would get done even while she was thinking and praying.

One of the things she looked forward to in her future with Jim was the opportunity to spend time reading Scripture and praying with him every day. She'd been doing it by herself for so long that she found she enjoyed it immensely when they shared it. Both were early risers by nature, so it would become a scheduled part of their morning routine.

She chastised herself for planning for married life with Jim when he hadn't even popped the question yet. But it was a foregone conclusion. They'd done a lot of talking about their future life together, but nothing close to a proposal had been made. That suited her. It had taken her a long time to get used to the idea of marrying again. In fact, for a long time it had kept her from even admitting to herself her deep feelings for Jim. But now she couldn't imagine a future without him.

Prayer was on her mind this morning too. She found herself thinking of the many people she'd been so intensely involved with the day before. Was it possible she had known Angela Liachi only one day? And Nathalie Benedict? She'd worked with Martin Grom before, but she'd never seen him near the edge like yesterday. Even Lionel Whalum came to mind, a man so removed from her life-style that she didn't know where to begin to pray for him.

141

How should she pray for such people? Not one of them, as far as she knew, was a church-goer, though some had indicated a certain God-consciousness. She guessed that that was where she should start, praying that God would somehow impress Himself upon them, get them thinking, make them receptive.

And then she prayed for opportunities to talk to them. She didn't know if she'd ever even see Lionel Whalum again, but she would undoubtedly see Martin Grom. And she could make it a point to see Mrs. Benedict and Angela. She knew she had something they needed, and she knew God could give her the words that could draw them to Himself.

Angela seemed especially sensitive, just by her nature and personality and by what she had been going through for the past several months. But someone else was tugging at the recesses of Jennifer's mind, and when she stopped for a minute and forced it to the surface, she knew immediately. Bobby Block.

There was no doubt he had got what he deserved. And it was probably the best thing that had ever happened to him. Not only had he been crushed by being fired, but when his ridiculous claims and conclusions about Jennifer were proved false, which would probably happen this very day, he would look like a fool.

She prayed that God would give her the resources to not retaliate. To show Bobby either by her silence or by the right word, should their paths cross, that she bore no grudges, that she wished him no further humiliation.

She knew if she could somehow glue together the loose ends in her mind this morning and if everything came together to support her wild hunches, she would not only play a major role in solving this latest development in the Heather Lauren-Wyatt Oliver murders, but she could also clear away all suspicion about herself.

She hoped that whatever happened would provide opportunities for her to interact with the principals of the case on a less emotional and rushed basis. *And I hope Jim is praying about this column decision,* she thought, *because I don't even have the time to think about it.*

Except that down deep she wanted to graduate to that job more than anything she had wanted in a long time. *I'll have to remind Jim to pray for my humility,* she decided. *Getting this thing out of perspective or thinking it's something I deserve can be dangerous.*

She snapped on her watch. Only a few minutes to spare. One last look in the mirror on her way to the hall cupboard showed her furry boots, corduroy Levis, a couple of layers of blouses and sweaters, topped by a cardigan buttoned all the way to the neck. She added a woollen hat and a down filled ski jacket and pulled on her mittens on the lift — after pushing the buttons.

She nodded and smiled to the doorman, who sat looking as if he were ready for bed. He looked surprised to see her again so soon, but he didn't ask any questions. The morning was even colder than Jennifer expected, shocking her fully awake as she swung out the door, notepads tucked under her arm.

'How can you look so good so early in the morning after such a short night?' Jim said as she slid into the car. 'I'm dead.'

'Ah, we're both dead,' she said, 'but you don't look so bad yourself.' Except for the colours, they were dressed almost alike.

'Where we goin'?' he asked.

'Head toward West Stivers,' she said. 'I'll be reading to you as we go.'

'It won't take long, this time of the morning,' he said. 'Read fast.'

She did. She sped through both notepads, reading everything she'd written, commenting on most of it, and adding titbits here and there from memory. Then she recounted the entire conversation she and Gerry Mayfield had had with Captain Halliday the night before, including all the exchanges between Halliday and Hank Henry.

'How can you remember all that, Jennifer?'

'I work on it. It's fun. I've always been able to do it. The only thing I regret about last night is that I agreed not to use any of the Halliday stuff in the paper. Would make great copy, don't you think?'

'Yeah. Now what do you want me to think about it? Much of it was new to me; some of it wasn't. I heard a few interesting things, but for the sake of time — that is if there's something

you want to do before the sun comes up —
you'd better coach me a little.'

'Well, what is it you've always told me about
investigative work? Haven't you said it's the
little things that slip past the first time, the
seemingly insignificant things, the apparently
unrelated things that wind up making the dif-
ference?'

'Yeah. It's always amazing how the things
you hear somehow fit together. Later they make
sense and you wonder how you almost missed
them, but most people do anyway. Did you
hear something that you think no one else
picked up on? That's the type of thing that'll
break this case.'

'I tried to recite the stuff to you straight, Jim,
without any inflection to give away what I
think is significant. Did you pick up anything?'

'Not really, but then I'm not really awake
yet.'

So she went back and selectively read and
recited various elements to see if he agreed
they fitted together. By his movement and tone
of voice, she could tell he was warming to her
speculations.

'First,' she said, 'settle in your mind who
might have had access to the schedule on
which Social Services takes people shopping.
The murderer had to know that.'

'Right, OK.'

'Then consider this: Angela Liachi may have
been a viable suspect early on because of her
threat, which had been on record. And she had
been seen in the neighbourhood, as I had. But

neither of us were really solid suspects after the forensics finished their work and after West Side homicide detectives had talked to the neighbours.'

'True enough. So?'

'Well, after the autopsy, when the angle of the puncture wounds and the strength needed to inflict wounds to that back muscle and rib cage was determined, we were both in the clear.'

'Right, and after the forensics determined the shoe size of the foot that kicked open Oliver's door, I gotta think Halliday and Grom and Henry are looking for a big man.'

'Yeah, but they may be looking too far.'

'I don't follow you, Jenn.'

'Don't you think Angela and I were scapegoats for a while?'

'You may be; she was a solid suspect for long enough. And scapegoats for whom. You think they have a more solid suspect they're hiding?'

'Or protecting?'

'Hiding, I could see. Then they can reveal him at a press conference and take a lot of credit. Why would they protect a solid suspect?'

'Tell me this, Jim: why would Grom have arrested me at the office when his partner, Hank Henry, had already interviewed neighbours, three of whom said they had seen Oliver alive after they had seen me run from his building?'

'You said Henry was in the car when Grom

was in your office, so he had to have told Grom.'

'Sure he told him. Grom ignored it for some reason.'

'Maybe he thought you knew too much, or he wanted to punish you for harbouring Angela, whom he thought was the real murderer.'

Jim approached the Oliver apartment building on West Stivers. 'Pull around the side, Jim, but not in the alley. When I was in the alley last night, after being inside the building, I noticed only one place wide enough for a panel truck to fit. The driver could have pulled in and backed out, but he or she could not have driven all the way through the alley.'

'Jenn, that grey, panel truck type vehicle business came from one kid. No one else saw it come or go.'

'And what did you just tell me about little, insignificant pieces of evidence?'

'But does your whole case rest on whether that type of vehicle was in the alley?'

'Sort of.'

'So that's why you wanted the forensic kit? For tyre tracks?'

'Uh huh.'

'No guarantees in this weather. The ground could have been so hard that no tracks were left; of course, a vehicle that big might leave tracks anyway. But if the ground has thawed and refrozen since it was here — if it was here — we'll get nothing.'

Jim pulled the heavy case from the boot, and

he and Jennifer dropped to all fours with a torch and crawled into the alley from the north. Almost immediately Jim held up a hand to stop her. 'Wide tracks,' he whispered. 'You were right. There's no proof it's the same vehicle, but there couldn't be too many trucks that go back here. A garbage truck couldn't even fit in here. Hey, I can see the forensics have been here.'

'Yeah,' Jennifer said, 'but they don't know where to start looking for tyres to match the tracks.'

'And you do?'

'Of course, Jim. You think I'd get up this early otherwise?'

In minutes, Jim had mixed a special plastic epoxy and poured ten-inch squares on three different patches of good tracks. He also poured some in a print of a shoe heel. 'I got a C in fingerprinting,' he said. 'But I was really good on tyre tracks in frozen ground!'

He waited five minutes, then carefully peeled up the reverse images, which had the consistency of rubber. He also measured the distance between the tracks. As they headed back to the car, he said, 'Anything else?'

'Nope. Not unless you want to look for the prints of a woman who broke a boot heel back here, a little farther south in the alley.'

'It wouldn't be hard to find. Now where do we go?'

'First, Jim, tell me how difficult it would be for anyone in either Oliver's or Whalum's building to see a vehicle parked where you made the track impressions.'

He crept past a wooden fence behind a ramshackle garage. 'You're right,' he said. 'I doubt if you could see it from there even if you were watching for it.'

'But no one was watching for it.'

'How do you know that?'

'Because everyone except one kid was distracted by police activity in front of the Whalum residence. Hank Henry was there twenty minutes, giving Lionel a little heat, remember?'

'Yeah. What are you saying?'

'You'll see. Take me about three blocks north of the West Side Precinct station, and I'll keep track of how long it takes us. Just drive at the speed limit.'

15 Less than ten minutes later, Jim pulled up to the curb across from the Chevy dealer on North Lester Avenue. The sun was rising, and employees of the service department were pulling in to park.

When the big garage door opened, Jim drove in. 'You're a little early,' a young mechanic said. 'What can we do for you?'

'I need to talk to whoever worked on Sergeant Grom's van yesterday.'

'Is that the cop's, the big silver and grey job with the one-way windows?'

'That's the one.'

'Melvin!'

'Yeah!'

'Guy's got a question here about the cop's van!'

Melvin, who was already greasy with the day hardly begun, hurried over. 'Who's askin'?'

'I am,' Jim said.

'You a friend of Grom's?'

'Yes.'

'Was there a problem? All we did was an oil change and lube job.'

'No problem. He's gonna settle up today, huh?'

'I guess so.'

'Can I see the invoice? I'll be seeing him this morning, and I can tell him how much.'

'Sure. I'll give you his copy.'

The invoice showed that Grom had delivered the van a few minutes before eight o'clock in the morning, the previous day.

'He musta picked it up last night after closing, 'cause it was still here when I left.'

'When was the work done?'

'Oh, let's see. I finished his by noon.'

'You sure?'

'Yeah. Finished a Trans Am first, then Sarge's work comes next, every time.'

'I'm sure he appreciates it.'

'I hope so.'

Captain John Halliday did not appreciate being awakened by Jennifer Grey after such a short night. But when he heard what she and Jim had uncovered, he agreed to meet them at the West Side station.

He arrived less than a half hour later — unshaven, wearing work clothes under a red and black woollen hunting jacket, and having just dragged a comb through his white hair. 'This is terrible,' he kept saying, 'but let's not jump to any conclusions.'

When presented with all of Jennifer's reasoning, he propped both elbows up on his desk and held his head in his hands. He buzzed the desk. 'What have you got for Grom yesterday between three-thirty and four-thirty?'

'Just a minute, Cap. Ah, yeah, away from the office on foot. Coffee break.'

'Get Hank Henry on the line for me, will ya? Thanks.'

Jim and Jennifer sat silently, occasionally catching one another's eye, as Halliday slumped in his chair. The intercom crackled. 'Hank Henry on line two, Cap.'

Halliday grabbed the phone. 'Hank, I need you in here right away. Something's breakin' on the Oliver murder...I'll tell ya when you get here.'

Jennifer started to speak as they waited for Henry to arrive, but Jim put a finger to his lips. Halliday wandered up and down the corridors, reading messages he himself had posted on the walls, some of them years before, but which he probably hadn't noticed since.

When Hank Henry arrived, they all piled into Halliday's unmarked squad car for the drive to the Near North Side. Henry alternately nodded in recognition of the conclusions that were being drawn and shook his head at the realization that his boss was in terrible trouble.

At the modest home of Sergeant Martin Grom, the four stood on the porch and rang the bell. They could hear kids running through the living room and up and down the stairs. The TV was blaring.

The five-year-old girl answered the door. 'Hi, Jackie,' Jennifer said, eliciting a smile.

'Hi, Red,' Halliday said. 'Your daddy home?'

She ran to get him as her mother came to the door with a worried look. 'Good morning, John,' she said. 'Is something wrong? Marty's still in bed.'

'Just want to talk to him for a few minutes, Roberta. Can you get him?'

She turned to head up the stairs, but Martin was already coming down in a dressing-gown and slippers. He looked as if he hadn't slept. 'Throw a coat on, Martin,' Halliday suggested. 'Wanna talk to you out here a minute.'

Grom reached for a heavy parka from a hook by the door and pulled it on as he came out. 'Let's take a little walk,' Halliday suggested.

'I don't wanna walk around the neighbourhood in my nightclothes, Captain.'

'We aren't going far, Martin.'

Mrs. Grom shut the door slowly as the unusual fivesome walked awkwardly down the front path to the pavement, west a few dozen feet and back up the driveway toward the garage. Hank Henry looked as if he wished he could be anywhere else.

'Why did you arrest Mrs. Grey last night when you knew Henry had interviewed several neighbours who saw Oliver alive after she left him?'

Grom looked first at Hank, then at Halliday. 'I had my reasons.'

'I want to hear one.'

'She was harbouring another suspect.'

'The other suspect wasn't much better, Martin. Why did you send Hank to see Whalum yesterday?'

'We often hassle these known baddies, Cap'n. You know that.'

'Not in the middle of a murder investigation we don't. You sure you didn't send him as a decoy, something for the neighbours to watch while you did some business in the neighbourhood yourself?'

Grom stood with his shoulders hunched and his hands deep in his pockets, the icy wind whipping at his pyjama legs and bare ankles. His breath began to come in short gusts from his nose, his lips were pressed tight. He said nothing.

'You changed your clothes somewhere on the way to and from Oliver's place yesterday, did you, Martin?' Halliday pressed.

Grom couldn't hold his boss's gaze and looked at the ground. He began to tremble. Halliday continued.

'Our guys were supposed to be out this morning looking for a big guy, big feet, probably a blue-collar worker, maybe an old truck driving associate of Oliver's, somebody that mighta pulled a grey panel truck type of a vehicle into the alley behind his place.'

Grom took his hands from his pockets and covered his face. 'But the tracks from that alley aren't gonna fit some panel truck somewhere, are they Martin? We can call off our guys, the ones who would have been reporting to you today, can't we?'

Grom began to weep.

'You wanna open the garage door for us, Martin, and let us measure the wheelbase and compare the track moulds and maybe look around in there for a big pair of bloody shoes, maybe some gloves, maybe some work clothes?'

Grom shook his head.

'We don't have to do that, Martin? You gonna save us the trouble? You wanna admit that you wore your uniform yesterday so people on Stivers wouldn't recognize you as the same guy who'd come through the back yard in the middle of the afternoon? And that you borrowed your own van from the Chevy garage during your coffee break so it would look like it had been at the garage all day?'

Grom nodded, sobbing, as his wife emerged from the back door to embrace him. He nearly collapsed in her arms. 'If only that Lauren woman had told me the truth on Wednesday!' he wailed. 'If only she'd said then that he had murdered the girl, this wouldn't have been necessary!'

'You'll have to get dressed and come with us, Martin,' Halliday said sadly.

'He was going to get off scot-free!' Grom moaned. 'I couldn't let that happen!'

Epilogue

Today I write a column I'd rather not write. In fact it's a column I will never want to remember, but shall never be able to forget.

Today I saw a man's life and career disintegrate, a man who had given himself in service for his community and his family for years. Two days ago he told me, 'If I had it my way, I'd kill Wyatt Oliver right now,' and then begged me not to quote him. I didn't, but it no longer matters.

Yesterday he had it his own way, and today he confessed to the slaying of a child killer. A father himself, Chicago Police West Side Homicide Detective Sergeant Martin Grom will face the penalty for taking the law into his own hands, for giving up on the system, for plotting and carrying out his own form of justice....